Undertow

Even though he was killing to be safe, not for pleasure. Three times within twenty-four hours. The warder; Guerrero; now this old man. Even after eight years in prison, that would have to be enough; now he must discipline himself, ration out the deaths, for that was the only way to keep it pleasurable. Three within twenty-four hours, but all three of them men; that was probably why he still felt unsatisfied. Eight years, eight long years to be paid for. Even so, it was wise to be careful . . .

The old man lay on the side of the path, the fingers of his right hand buried in the soft earth. Moreno kicked him lightly in the ribs with his black cloth shoes as he stepped past, then picked up the canvas bag and slung it over his shoulder. He set off down the path, whistling softly as he went; Cara al Sol, the National Hymn of the Falangists. He had no sense of humor, but he appreciated irony.

Other titles in the Walker British Mystery Series

DESMOND CORY
Undertow

WALKER AND COMPANY · NEW YORK

First published in the United States of America
in 1963 by the Walker Publishing Company, Inc.

This paperback edition first published in 1983.

ISBN: 0-8027-3044-2

Library of Congress Catalog Card Number: 63-11471

Printed in the United States of America

10   9   8   7   6   5   4   3   2   1

UNDERTOW

JUAN Guerrero lay face down on the stiff, rutted clay to one side of the road, and a small black beetle crawled over the palm of his hand. Guerrero took no notice. He wore the loose grey uniform that is issued to all inmates of Franco's prisons; the cuffs were rucked back to show his thin forearms, grey with the pallor of the jail, furred with tiny black hairs.

Juan Guerrero was dead. There was a small wound at the base of his throat, a wound that had been made by something like a meat skewer; something that had penetrated the sinews of his neck and severed the carotid artery. Guerrero had fallen to his knees and had then pitched forward, and the rough soil had torn open the skin of his nose and forehead; he had felt no pain, though. He had been dead already. The artery had continued pulsing for twenty seconds or a little less, spouting his blood on to the dry Spanish soil; but the earth had long since swallowed it up and now nothing was left but a dark circular stain, about three feet in diameter, in the centre of which his head rested. A stain like a black halo.

The tall man with the camera stood up and nodded, and the two men who had been watching him stooped down and turned Guerrero over. The tall man leaned forward; the impassive eye of the camera lens stared at the tiny puncture in Guerrero's neck. A sudden blink of sharp white light, a click. The tall man changed the flash bulb, took another shot from a different angle. His movements were unhurried, unconcerned.

In the end he dismantled the flash carrier, snapped the camera into its case and turned casually away towards the waiting SEAT four-seater. The other two men followed, ten paces behind him. The car doors slammed noisily in the throbbing evening stillness; after a moment's pause, the engine picked up and the car drove off. A fine white powdery dust drifted up into the air, and grains of it settled on Guerrero's crumpled body.

"EXCELLENT," said Acuña. "Excellent."

He pushed the photographs across the desk. Valera picked them up, holding them lightly between his fingertips, and tilted them towards the window. "Yes," he said, staring at them. "Excellent. What was the weapon?"

"We don't know. Something he improvised. A ground-down bed-spring, perhaps, or something like that. It hardly matters. Look where he placed it— that's the point. He hasn't lost his touch."

Valera looked up. "You seem almost pleased about it."

"Quite the contrary. But one must admire professional competence whenever one comes across it."

Acuña pushed back his chair and stood up. Acuña was a small man with a heavy paunch, so heavy that he seemed to roll himself forward rather than to walk; he had his chin lowered to his chest and his hands thrust deep into his pockets, and both these factors contributed to the effect. The top of his sunken head was big and round and bald and polished. There was something slightly obscene about Acuña. People rarely felt at ease in his presence. The discomfort he caused them was purely physical; his job had nothing to do with it. Only a handful of people knew what his job was.

Valera knew, but Valera was one of the few men on whom Acuña's personal appearance made no impression at all. Valera was a policeman, part of a very large machine; he had grown accustomed to treating of his superior officers as components of the same mechanism, all performing their functions with greater or less efficiency. And if he ever felt a certain revulsion towards his role as Acuña's chief assistant, he never showed it.

Acuña was in fact a mass murderer. In the twenty-odd years since the Spanish Civil War had ended, he had killed nearly three thousand men and women. Death had been the punishment for crimes of which, nine times out of ten, they had been no more than technically guilty; this Acuña knew as well as anyone, but . . . he believed in making sure. He knew very little for certain. All that he knew was that somewhere in that vast pile of three thousand mouldering corpses lay the bodies of seventy-six of the Soviet Union's most expert and highly-trained spies and saboteurs, and with their bodies so much else. . . . Long years of arduous labour in the *Agitprop* schools, hours of expert instruction of other spies, a whole vast series of events that had never taken place—burning factories, crashing aircraft, nationwide strikes, unexpected assassinations. That was all that Acuña knew. He didn't even know exactly which were the seventy-six bodies that counted. It didn't matter much. They knew in Moscow.

They knew in Moscow, all right. They knew that in Western Europe there was one man, at least, who had learnt their own methods of total extermination and who put them to violent practice. But they didn't know who it was. Four men of the seventy-six had been sent to Madrid to find out. They had failed to do so. They had died. And Acuña, meanwhile, lived; a bald, greasy man like a bladder of lard, sending out his executioners to prisons and to private houses all over Spain. A man much hated, but rarely despised.

Valera put the photographs down on the desk again. Face downwards. "Poor sod," he said. "Poor sod."

"Three years in prison. First in Valencia, then in Sevilla. Nine months building up his friendship with Moreno. Step by step, inch by inch. Never a false move. Treated like all the other convicts. Waiting for the move. All right. Then it comes. Then the escape. Not the slightest detail goes astray. One of the warders has to die, even, to make the escape more convincing. And then . . . two hours later. . . ." Acuña wheeled his belly up to the desk, speared the photographs down on the desk's surface with one fat forefinger. ". . . Moreno kills him. For no reason whatsoever. Other than that he likes killing, that it's what he does best in the world. And it had to be Juan—one of the best men I've ever had, if that means anything. Probably never even tried to defend himself. He knew Moreno had to go free. So he let himself be killed. By an animal. What a way to die. *Hijo de la puta*."

Valera shrugged. "More likely he never saw it. Moreno wouldn't have given him any sort of a chance."

"Well, there it is. It makes things a lot more difficult."

Acuña took a pink-tipped cigarette from the silver case on the desk, accepted the flame from Valera's proferred lighter. "He'll kill again," he said matter-of-factly. "He's bound to. And we have to give the news to the press. If he gets to see a newspaper and there's no mention of the killings, he's bound to smell a rat. We have to treat him exactly like any other escaped killer, because if we don't, we give the game away. All-station police alerts, the whole caboodle. It can't be helped."

"They won't catch him. Not Moreno."

"They might if he were alone. They might just. But I'm hoping that after today he won't be."

They stared together at the large-scale map of Southern Spain that hung on the far wall. An unusual map; a map worth anything in the region of five thousand pounds. That, at any rate, was the price that the Soviet External Intelligence Service had offered for it and might, under certain circumstances, even have been willing to pay. "Here's where they jumped for it," said Acuña flatly, "and here's where Guerrero bought it. Nine kilometres farther south, or so. Inference, that they were headed for Malaga." His finger pointed now towards the profusion of red-circled dots that showed the whereabouts of known and of suspected Communist centres; he withdrew his hand, and a very fine sapphire ring winked momentarily in the sun. "By now, he'll be moving through the mountains towards the coast, towards just about any point between Malaga and Torre del Mar. That's how *I* read it."

He went on looking at the map. At the road that twisted over the dull grey wastes of the Sierra de Malaga. Lonely country, rocky country, wooded country. Country where, for one man, an army could search in vain. And the man they called Moreno knew that country, knew it well. "He'll have a contact, I suppose," said Valera thoughtfully.

"Of course he'll have a contact."

"Well, it's all right. He's doing what we wanted."

"Yes, but we wanted Guerrero on the spot. We wanted to give them Moreno, yes, but not on a plate."

He looked at Valera expressionlessly. His great round forehead was shiny with sweat. "We've let loose the wolf all right," he said. "And now he's going to join the pack. All we have to know is *where*." He turned away abruptly, as though no longer interested.

". . . You'd better get down there," he said. "Don't you think?"

To the west of the village, the olive trees gave way to the rock and to the rough red earth. The slope grew very steep; a zigzag path led down it. Then, at the foot of the hill, the olive trees moved off again all together, stretching in long low ranks towards the south, and the red earth heaved slowly up beneath them in a massive shoulder that shrugged round to the west and down to the sea. Beyond that last upthrust of the hills, beyond and out of sight, was the flat land, the sugar-cane and maize fields of the Malaga coast. To the north lay the mountains, grey as ash and hard of outline, severe and menacing; the village was nearer, a tiny cluster of white walls and brown roofs balanced on the lap of the hill, precariously, as though the slightest of movements would send it slithering and sliding a full half-mile to pile up at last in rubble amongst the olive trees below. The two men who sat on the rough stone wall to one side of the path were facing the village, yet never raised their heads to look at it. Nor did they look at each other. For the most part, they stared over the olive groves towards the sea.

The elder of the two would have attracted no one's attention against such a background. An Andalusian *campesino*, with a widebrimmed straw hat, sunbleached trousers and a grey cotton tunic that he wore loose, buttoned only at the neck. His face seemed hardly a face so much as a nest of wrinkles, of great folded creases, running into one another and branching away again, complex as a Chinese puzzle; in the deepest slits of all were set two pebbles the colour of dry brick, dark and unwinking. His voice, when he spoke, was hardly intelligible; its rasp seemed to strangle all vowels at birth so that nothing emerged but consonants grinding against each other like slabs of granite in a glacier.

The man who listened to him would, on the other hand, have attracted attention anywhere. He, too, wore the clothes of a southern farm labourer, the drab shirt and colourless trousers and off-white vest; but totally failed to look the part. His body was magnificent as that of an Uffizi Perseus, heavy yet lithe, bulky yet smoothly-muscled, with wide shoulders and long, powerful arms, tight buttocks and compact stomach, carrying hardly an ounce of superfluous fat; while the skin had a cold, pallid translucence like that of marble, emphasising the body's resemblance to some classic sculpture. Moreno's hair was dark and cut very short; his chin jutted from the firm, rounded muscles of his neck; his eyes were light brown and his mouth was wide and insensitive. As a farm hand, Moreno looked absurd; and if he was, as Acuña had claimed, an animal, this was hardly surprising. Animals rarely look their best when clothed. In his natural state, though, Moreno was undeniably a very fine-looking animal indeed.

"Yes," he said, when the old man had finished talking. "I understand all that."

"All you got t'do is wait. .Wait till the boat comes, see? Never mind if it's late. They said not to worry."

"I never worry," said Moreno.

"Right y'are, then. You got the clothes now an' you got some food. You won't be wantin' me for anything else." ·

"There wasn't any message, then?"

"What?"

"There wasn't any message?"

The words seemed to hold no special intonation, but the old man turned his head to look at Moreno. Then Moreno sat on the wall and watched him until his legs stopped twitching. . . . Then the light died slowly from Moreno's brown eyes and he reached up a hand to wipe away the saliva that had coursed down from the corners of his lips. Three, he told himself. That will have to be enough. . . .

Even though he was killing to be safe, not for pleasure. Three times within twenty-four hours. The warder; Guerrero; now this old man. Even after eight years in prison, that would have to be enough; now he must discipline himself, ration out the deaths, for that was the only way to keep it pleasurable. Three within twenty-four hours, but all three of them men; that was probably why he still felt unsatisfied. Eight years, eight long years to be paid for. Even so, it was wise to be careful. . . .

The old man lay on the side of the path, the fingers of his right hand buried in the soft earth. Moreno kicked him lightly in the ribs with his black cloth shoes as he stepped past, then picked up the canvas bag and slung it over his shoulder. He set off down the path, whistling softly as he went; *Cara al Sol*, the National Hymn of the Falangists. He had no sense of humour, but he appreciated irony.

His feet moved a trifle awkwardly on the rough

stones; not shuffling, but not with a countryman's ease. In prison he had kept himself as fit as he could, which was very fit indeed; but his legs were still unused to any but flat surfaces and it would be some little time, as he guessed, before they grew accustomed to the change. It hadn't prevented him from making good speed across the sierra, and he expected no trouble from this the final stage.

He walked on through the olive trees. He had no watch, but by the heat and by the angle of the sun he knew that it was still the siesta hour; he would meet nobody in the olive groves, nobody awake. He stayed alert, though, for the sight of sleeping bodies in the shade. He saw none. Eventually the path forked, as the old man had said it would, and he took the right-hand branch that turned towards the sea. The armpits and the back of his shirt were darkened already with sweat, but he did not relax his pace. He was in a hurry, but not because he was afraid. He was quite calm and confident. He was Moreno. *They* would never catch him.

HE reached the coast well before the sun had reached the hard blue line of the horizon. He had two hours, at least, to spare. He stood amongst the sand dunes looking down at the bay of which the old man had spoken, at the rocky promontory with the umbrella pines, at the line of foam left behind by the slow-moving waves as they lapped against the beach. It was a beautiful scene and Moreno was sensitive to beauty. Indeed, he found after a while that he was crying. He felt at once sad and exultant. In eight years, he hadn't seen the sea.

Now it was there before him, and he knew exactly what he wanted to do. In the old days, what Moreno wanted and what Moreno did had been always one and the same thing. And now he was Moreno once again. He slipped off his clothes, ran swiftly down to the water's edge and plunged in.

Anyone watching him at that moment might have thought that he had been returned, like a fish, to his native element. The slight clumsiness that had marked his movements on land instantly disappeared, was lost in the smooth, powerful roll of his shoulders and the kicking thrust of his thighs. He went through the clear green-blue water like an arrow, diving and surfacing again and again; went deeper, and then there was a whiteness flitting like a phantom over the ribs of sand beneath the waves. Two hundred yards out, he turned

over on his back and floated, as totally and uncon-
cernedly relaxed as a seagull; then arched himself into
a sudden parabola of twisting muscle and headed fast
for the shore, travelling with that deceptively lazy
Australian crawl stroke that swirled a foaming wake
behind it like that of a speedboat. Back on land, he ran
to where he had left his clothes and lay down to dry
himself in the sun. His great body gleamed like pearl,
like the nacre inside a seashell. Eight years ago, it had
been tanned almost to a negro's darkness; already it was
responding to the touch of the sea and the sun, held the
most delicate possible of pink undertones. Though the
sun itself was now sinking fast. . . .

At sunset, Moreno rose and dressed himself and
moved off once more, the blue canvas bag in his right
hand. Amongst the pine trees on the little promontory,
he settled himself down again; took from the bag a loaf
of bread, Manchego cheese, a bottle of olive oil and
another of red wine. He ate and drank, chewing the
food with a pedantic thoroughness, while the light
slowly bled from the sky. The sands of the beach held a
luminosity for some time after the sun had finally sunk;
but after a while that uncertain paleness faded and the
stars came out, strong and clear, in a night of humming
velvet. Moreno corked the wine bottle and replaced it
in the bag; of the bread and cheese and oil, not a scrap
remained. He lay stretched out in the darkness com-
fortably as a cat, waiting. The lights of a fishing-boat
a mile or so away interested him for several minutes;
but they drifted east with the current and, long before
they finally disappeared, he had ceased to watch them.
In the end, he closed his eyes, choosing to rely entirely
on his ears.

For what seemed a very long time, he heard nothing. Nothing but the gentle sound of the sea breeze in the pine needles overhead and the lapping, scarcely louder, of the waves on the rocks beneath. Until at last he heard a sound unlike the other sounds, and he listened more intently in order to be sure, and when he was perfectly sure he opened his eyes and sat up. He heard then more distinctly the faint squeaking of oars on rowlocks, and in the water he could see a vague phosphorescence moving slowly in towards the shore. Eventually he heard the grind and crunch as the boat beached itself on the sands. Then he got up and made his way, silently, to where the two men were waiting.

He said nothing to them, because there was nothing to be said. They were unimportant. They knew who he was and they were afraid of him; he sensed their fear as he clambered into the boat. Their feet splashed noisily in the water as they pushed off, and their breathing was loud in the stillness. Out of condition, obviously. Why? *They* hadn't been in jail. Now they began to pull at the oars and the boat to respond, dancing a little to the movement of the waves. The saltness of the open sea, striking at the nostrils; Moreno couldn't repress a little shudder of delight. He stretched himself out on the hard wooden seat, feeling the waves slap, slap, slap, very gently, against the hull; very gently, very quietly; as though breaking on his own proferred body, cradling it, lulling it. For the first time since he had escaped, he felt that he would like to go to sleep.

No time for sleep now, though. The yacht was little more than four hundred yards out. He didn't see it until they were almost up against it; then it was a sudden black bulk shutting out the sky to the south, and a masked torch was winking at him from somewhere on the deck. The boat drifted in on the undertow; the torch winked again, and one of the oarsmen growled under his breath. "Rope ladder down the side," he said to Moreno. "See if you can spot it. Can't give you any light."

"I don't need any," said Moreno. He was on his feet already, his legs braced against the slow rocking of the swell. The boat touched the yacht's fenders once and then again, grinding in harder. He saw the ladder then, a spidery shadow creeping down towards him; he reached out, felt the rough wood of one of the treads rasp against his palm, and instantly swung himself upwards. That was another knack that he hadn't lost. . . . He mounted swiftly, swung his leg over the guardrail and landed on the deck. The man waiting at the top of the ladder took him by the elbow as if to help him . . . let go of it at once as though it were red-hot. "Everything okay?"

"Everything," said Moreno.

"Good," said the other man. "*Venez avec.*"

Moreno followed him across the empty deck down brass-nailed steps, through a white-painted door with a window of frosted glass. Inside, a spotless passage, a soft green carpet. A luxury yacht, then. He had suspected as much already. Halfway down the passage, the Frenchman stopped, opened a door. "Your cabin," he said.

A tiny cabin, not more than eight feet by five. A folding bunk ran the full length of the opposite bulkhead; it had been made up with clean sheets and a white wool blanket. On a shelf above it stood an alarm clock, a handful of paperbacked books, a mirror, shaving gear. Moreno tapped his finger against the card in a neat metal slot beside the door; *Jaime Baroda*, it said. "Who's Jaime Baroda?"

"You are Jaime Baroda."

Moreno nodded rather tiredly. He picked up the photograph in the red leather frame that stood at the head of the bunk; a pleasant-looking old couple smiling arm-in-arm at the camera. "And who are these?"

The Frenchman smiled, too. "No doubt they will be your parents."

"I see," said Moreno. "Amusing."

He didn't really find it amusing. Just familiar; half-forgotten, yet completely familiar. Someone else's possessions were already his; he felt himself at home, more so than if his own name had been on the door. "These things will be explained to you in the morning," said the Frenchman. "Meanwhile you are free to sleep."

Moreno looked at him. A small, thickset man of about his own age, with black curly hair and a hairline moustache. A neat white shirt and, in spite of the heat, a carefully-knotted silk bow tie. In the eyes, a slight opaqueness; the opaqueness of fear. This man was afraid of him, too; another thing that Moreno didn't really find amusing. The warders at Valencia, at Sevilla—they also had been afraid of him; he disliked finding their expression in the eyes of this stranger. "What's your name?" he said.

"Meuvret. Charles Meuvret. Not that it matters."

"You own this yacht?"

"No, no. I just help to run it."

Moreno sat down on the bunk, swung his legs up to

the mattress. "Perhaps I shall sleep now," he said. His tone was of dismissal.

"Yes, do that. The chief will see you in the morning."

Moreno closed his eyes. He heard the door click shut; listened intently for the sound of a key turning. It didn't come. That would have been childish, anyway. But childish was what these people so often were. Thorough, competent . . . but childish. He unfastened the strings of his shoes, kicked them away from him. These people . . . they wanted something, of course. Probably something that he knew. He knew so many things, so many secrets. He had been put in prison for knowing too much. Not for killing, no. The murders had merely given them their excuse. Now he was free. And very tired. Now and at last he could go to sleep.

FERAMONTOV watched through the narrow metal spyhole until one of the great hands relaxed and slithered down to the mattress, until Moreno's chest—visible through the open gap of his shirt—was stirring with the gentle regularity of sleep. Then he watched patiently, placidly, expressionlessly, for five minutes more. When he sensed the hull of the yacht beginning to vibrate to the turning-over of its engines, he pulled down the strip of steel that masked the Judas window and fastened the catch. "He hasn't changed much," he said. "Hardly at all. But Spanish prisons can mark a man in many ways, you know. . . . Till I've spoken to him, I can't be sure."

The girl took a test-tube from the rack opposite her, shook it, held it up to the light. She seemed absorbed entirely in her work; her face was cold, abstracted. Blunt nose, wide cheekbones, deep-set blue eyes, and a frame of jet-black hair; a face that, even in its intentness, held more than a promise of open sensuality. It made the white, impersonal chemist's smock that she wore seem actually provocative; the long sleeves and high-buttoned neck, the air of scientific puritanism in which —looking at that face—nobody could seriously believe for more than a moment. Feramontov glanced briefly towards her, then went to sit in the foam-rubber armchair directly behind her. This position afforded him an excellent view of her legs, and Feramontov liked looking at her legs, especially her ankles. Russian women are inclined to thickness at the ankle—to thickness everywhere, in fact. Feramontov had learnt Western tastes, in women as in almost everything else.

He himself looked hardly at all like a Russian, and this he counted as an asset in his profession. Feramontov looked rather like a cat; though if you tried to pin down the resemblance, you would probably have to decide that it was one of behaviour rather than of personal appearance. Feramontov *moved* like a cat; he had a cat's perfect economy of muscular effort and a cat's gift of relaxation, while his gaze was as calm and dispassionate as a tiger's, never seeming to do more than estimate the distance between himself and other objects in pouncing terms. Kings, fools, courtesans, killers—all were rendered alike by the impersonality of his steady green stare, were reduced to common factors, to ciphers. And if it is possible to discern cruelty in the ordinary bodily movements of a man, then all Feramontov's actions were innate with it.

This, though he had no clear understanding of the meaning of the word. He was cruel by nature, as a tiger is cruel; and cowardly by nature, as a lion is cowardly. Cowardice to him was caution, and caution was wisdom; where a slight scratch can hinder one's hunting for many days afterwards, it's wise to be cautious of beasts with horns. Only British sportsmen consider the lion a coward for that reason; and whatever else Feramontov might have been, he was no British sportsman. He hunted not as a pastime, but for his livelihood. He was a professional, in a word. Cruel, cautious and clever. Clever enough never to examine himself in such terms, clever enough to let other people worry about what abstract qualities he possessed or didn't possess. They did. Many people did. But for Feramontov, it was enough simply to be alive and hunting.

With the girl, he spoke German. That was her native language. But they could have conversed as easily in Russian, English, French, Spanish or Italian. Soviet secret operatives are better linguists than most. "We're all near-lunatics now," said Feramontov, "every one of us. The trouble with Moreno may just be that he's a bit too normal. He does what comes naturally. And anyone who does that all the time is obviously a danger to society. To society in general, and to our organisation in particular. I wish I could feel happier about Moreno."

The girl still gave no sign of having heard him. She raised another test-tube to the light in her silver-tipped fingers, studied it closely. It contained an almost colourless liquid with undertones of green—sea water— and tiny white hairlike objects drifted to and fro within it. "He likes to kill," she said eventually. "And he's said to be intelligent. But you've dealt with killers before. And with intelligent ones."

"Oh, yes. A hundred others. But Moreno. . . . " Feramontov considered in silence for a moment. "*Er war anders.*"

The girl shrugged. She replaced the tube in the rack, then walked across to the spyhole and freed its metal cover. The white overall rustled softly as she leaned forward. She looked into the little cabin for perhaps thirty seconds, then straightened her slim back again and lowered the cover. "A very fine physique," she said. "Quite magnificent."

"Yes. They so often have."

"Good looking, as well."

Feramontov smiled tightly. "It serves no practical purpose. He isn't interested in women. Except, of course, in connection with his little hobby."

"A pity, in some ways." The girl went back to her test-tubes, though now she stood facing Feramontov. "I won't be of much use to you, in that case."

"What's the matter? Anxious for promotion?"

"One wishes to be useful."

"Sometimes, it's enough to be decorative. You're always that." Feramontov watched her; no hint of speculation in his eyes, no desire, nothing; just an unwavering greenness, pale almost as the water in the test-tubes. And after a moment, the girl turned away. "Perhaps," said Feramontov, "we may let him carve you up some night when there's a full moon. That's if he's a *very* good boy."

"A joke in very poor taste."

"My jokes often are. I have excellent taste, though . . . in other directions."

The girl lowered infinitesimally her fine black eyebrows. She took a pencil from her pocket, began to make notes on the pad that lay open on the desk. "*Ja, mit Frauen umzugehen. Ich verstehe.*"

"We understand each other very well." Feramontov rose smoothly to his feet. "As it happens, I have news of the Professor. There may well be work for you, in Marbella."

"There's always work for the Professor."

"Of a different kind. There are two Englishmen staying at the Spyglass. *Young* Englishmen. You may have to make yet another sacrifice for the Party."

"Two at once?" said the girl; and, for the first time, smiled. "It sounds positively Roman."

She clipped the pencil back into her pocket, moved away round the long wooden rack. Feramontov followed her, not closely. They stared together into the deep tank let into the floor at their feet, a big metal tank with a glass cover. Within was a yellow-green light, soft, hypnotic, and in that light numberless shadowy forms pulsed and pulullated; raw red gashes opened and closed like festering wounds, feathery tentacles writhed. The tank was full of jellyfish. ·

"Your little pets," said Feramontov, but didn't smile.

"Yes, my little pets. On the whole, I prefer them to Englishmen. To any other men, for that matter."

They moved in the depths of the tank as in a yellow-green nightmare. Swollen blubbery bells, swinging their poison-laden feelers through the water. Feramontov wetted his lips with the tip of his tongue. He hated to admit it, but those jellyfish were amongst the few things of which he was genuinely afraid. "You look after them well," he said. "Better than most women do their husbands."

"If I didn't, they'd probably die," said the girl. "Which would be a pity."

"Of course. Now I, too, have certain things to attend to."

The girl didn't turn her head to watch him leave. She was checking the temperature of the water; her face again calm, unsmiling as before. Only when the door had closed did her expression relax; she closed her eyes for a second, resting her hands on the brown polished surface of the rack. While in the tank beneath her, stealthily, the jellyfish swam to and fro. . . .

THEY came in while Moreno was finishing his breakfast and sat down at the table. Meuvret, whom he knew already. A thin man, fair-haired, with a curious delicacy of movement. And a girl, dark and beautiful, who wore a blue flannel wrap over a bathing costume. They sat down at the breakfast table with its fleecy white tablecloth and its plates of Meissen porcelain, and the man in the white jacket who had been standing by the door went unobtrusively out. "Good morning," said the man who moved like a cat. "Sleep well?"

Moreno nodded without looking up; he was pouring himself out a second cup of coffee. "I was tired."

"That was to be expected. For that reason, I chose to postpone our little discussion until this morning. You don't know me, by any chance?"

Moreno looked at him without curiosity, then shook his head.

"But perhaps you know *of* me. Feramontov."

"Feramontov. . . . Yes. Barcelona, forty-four."

"Exactly. A long time ago, of course. I'm glad you still retain your excellent memory. However, you won't know this young lady; she's from Germany. Her name is Elsa."

Moreno nodded, again without looking at her face. Faces told one nothing; he preferred to watch hands and bodies. The girl's hands, he noticed, were lightly

clenched; Feramontov's were out of sight under the
table. Feramontov knew a thing or two. Moreno's eyes
moved back to the girl's body, stayed there. This one
has control, he thought, but she can't relax. She's never
learnt how to. That's what happens to women in this
kind of work. She's young still, young enough to learn;
but if not, she'll have to be got rid of. Yes, indeed, he
thought; pleasant work if one could get it. . . .

"Meuvret, of course, you've already met."

Nothing in the tone to indicate that Feramontov
knew what he was thinking, but Moreno was instantly
sure of it. He frowned; he disliked having his thoughts
read; they were part of himself, they were private. To
Meuvret, he didn't even nod. Meuvret was of no
importance.

"Now perhaps you'll tell us something of your
escape."

Moreno reached for his cup, drank a little coffee
before replying. "There's not very much to tell. I was
being moved from the prison at Sevilla to Malaga,
along with another fellow called Guerrero. The car
picked up a puncture in the hills near Colmenar,
swerved a bit. . . . We had half a chance and we took it.
We knew what to do because we'd discussed it before-
hand. I took one warder and Guerrero the other. Then
we took the driver. He had time to shout, but no one
heard."

"Yes. This Guerrero, who is he?"

"Armed robbery back in '57. It hardly matters,
though. He's dead now."

Moreno unhooked from his belt the six-inch long,
sharply pointed length of steel cable that one of the
convicts had smuggled out to him from the electricians'

workshop. He laid it on the table without lifting his eyes. "In prison one has to make do with what one can get. It turned out to be adequate."

"He was . . . difficult?"

"Difficult?" Moreno seemed uncertain as to what the word meant, exactly. "No. But you never can tell. I thought it best to make sure." He finished his coffee.

"And then?"

"I'd had your message, of course. I knew you were looking for me, that you'd have left word. So I travelled south. I saw Andres."

"Ah, Andres." Feramontov breathed deeply, softly.

"Yes. The old man. Again, I thought that the police might be behind me. . . . Dogs, witnesses, so many things. . . . I made sure."

"You made sure." Feramontov leaned back and his teeth gleamed for a second in the overhead light. "In short, you've been on the bash."

And Moreno smiled, too. "That's right," he said. "On the bash."

This, he knew, was the moment to look the girl full in the face. He did so. She was watching him, frowning and intent. There was curiosity in her eyes, but not the fear he had expected; her eyes might have been those of a research chemist, examining the behaviour of a bacillus on a glass slide. Instantly and unreasonably, he felt the pumping of anger inside his head; and knew at once that she sensed it in him, guessed at his hatred of her. Moreno hated all women, but most of all those for whom, had they been men, he might have felt a certain respect. Elsa now for him was more than merely a woman. She was an enemy.

"I see you are wearing one of the suits we prepared

for you," said Feramontov easily. "You find it comfortable?"

"Comfortable, yes. It has been worn before, though."

"Naturally."

"You think of everything."

"We try to. There is no question of preparing you against a detailed examination—we can't do anything about your fingerprints, at the moment—but that's no reason for making elementary errors. You won't be landing in Spain, at any rate officially, and the papers we are supplying you with will be good enough for Tangier. At the moment, therefore, there's no need to brief you too closely as to your cover story. Your name is Jaime Baroda, you are from Valencia and you are at present working under Meuvret here as a collector of specimens."

"Of what?"

"Of specimens. This yacht is under charter to the Association of Marine Biology in Monaco, and Meuvret is Director of the expedition. You are employed, in fact, as a skin diver."

Moreno spread out his hands on the table, palm downwards, and looked at them. "What do you want me for?" he said shortly.

Feramontov pushed aside a neatly-dismembered grapefruit, began to help himself to liver and bacon. "The Spanish branch of our Overseas Intelligence is very anxious to interview you, Baroda. You have certain information they'd be very happy to receive."

"I imagined there'd be something more specific."

"Yes. There is."

". . . Well?"

"We want the Spyglass logbooks."

"The Spyglass logbooks." Moreno nodded. "I see."

He was careful, very careful, not to show surprise. This wasn't what he had expected. Maybe it was a bluff, of course; maybe what they really wanted was something quite different. They could be just testing him to see how far he'd co-operate. "They'll still be there," he said.

"Hidden in the house?"

"Hidden . . . *near* the house."

"We've searched. We couldn't find them. We have to know exactly where they are."

"I know exactly where they are."

Feramontov laughed, suddenly and shortly. "Yes, your memory is excellent. That much has been proved. So that . . . if we take you to the house, you'll have no trouble in recovering those logbooks from where they're hidden?"

"None. Or very little. Does Priego still own the place?"

"Priego died two years ago. A heart attack."

"I didn't know."

"He left it to a friend of his, a South American called Tocino, who himself died last autumn. The death rate among capitalist millionaires is something that our propagandists might do well to dwell on. It now belongs to Tocino's daughter."

"Who is in South America?"

"Precisely. The house has been now either rented or borrowed by two Englishmen. There is a housekeeper and a maidservant, living at the back of the premises. I am hoping," said Feramontov, and smiled at Elsa, "that we can get the Englishmen out of the way for at least one evening. It should be no problem."

"For one evening or for ever. No problem at all."

"Killing should not be necessary," said Feramontov, "and is certainly not advisable. When the proper precautions have been taken, killing is rarely necessary." Moreno, sensing a threat that the words themselves hardly seemed to contain, felt his fingers curling up on the table; he dropped his hands unhurriedly to his lap. "You help us, Baroda, and we'll help you. That's the way it is."

He tilted back his chair, looked out through the nearest porthole. Blue sky, green-blue sea, and on the horizon a flat brown line of land; the coast of Spain. "You're a very fine swimmer, according to the records."

"Out of practice," said Moreno, not very clearly.

"Obviously. But you'll be able to get some practice in. Elsa is a good swimmer, too. She has been training with the Soviet team for the Olympic Games. We're all in favour, you see, of peaceful co-existence."

"That's since my time," said Moreno brusquely. "Two long words and what they mean is, *business as usual*. Or am I wrong?"

Feramontov carefully sliced the rind off a rasher of bacon. "My point is that *your* kind of business is not particularly usual," he said. Then, with the air of one who finds a given challenge not worth the trouble of taking up, he picked the makeshift dagger from the table and tested the point against his thumb. "Though it has to be admitted that there's what one might call a permanent demand. A permanent demand for a special talent."

"I've always found so," said Moreno, and smiled triumphantly.

"All the same, we'll have to get rid of this thing. It's

too distinctive. I have something new you may care to play with."

He wiped his mouth punctiliously on his napkin, got up and went over to the tall locker in the corner of the room. From it he took a peculiar contraption of steel, wood and rubber, a cross between a rifle and a catapult. "These, also, are since your time," he said casually. "You may never have seen one, but they've become extremely popular. And this is as powerful as any of its kind. Look."

He braced his feet on the floor, winding the tough pink rubber band back along the shaft. A metal catch clicked into place behind the trigger. Between the tensed rubber thongs was fitted a light wooden bolt with a barbed steel head. "A kind of catapult, you see. Or crossbow."

"What does it do?"

Feramontov raised the shaft, settling it against his hip, and pressed the trigger. His body jerked with the sudden whip of the recoil. A quick gasp of air, a splintering crack; the bolt quivered in the door, driven through the wood a half of its length from a range of twelve feet. Moreno stared at it open-mouthed. He hadn't expected that kind of power from so childish-looking a weapon. Then his eyes glinted as though filled with tears, and he reached out his hands.

"Yes," he said. "Here. Give it to me."

"It's for fish."

"I know. I've heard about them. Here. Let's see it."

Feramontov handed it to him. "Later," he said, "you can go down into the water and practise. It's not difficult. Elsa will teach you." He watched Moreno's dark head bowed over the long shaft, the rubber straps;

watched silently, impersonally, like a stalking cat. "She will make you a fisher of men," he said; and giggled.

"WEAPON nearly circular," said the police surgeon. His voice was dry and monotonous as the buzzing of the flies high up on the wall. "About a third of a centimetre in diameter and flexible. Penetration barely two centimetres, just enough to sever the artery. Trajectory dead level. In fact, a very neat job indeed. Straight, short and sweet."

He drew the rough linen sheet back over the creased and twisted face, then clicked his fingers. The mortuary assistant came forward to wheel the cadaver away. "I'll see the effects," said Valera.

"Over here, sir."

The sergeant of the Civil Guard opened a drawer, took out a knotted handkerchief. Valera waved him on as he fumbled for his cotton gloves. "Never mind the normal precautions," he said. "The prints have no bearing on the case."

"Very well, sir."

He unfastened the handkerchief. Inside was a half-empty packet of Ideal cigarettes, a crumpled matchbox, a cheap medallion on a broken chain, two cigarette stubs, a dirty cube of sugar, four filthy one-peseta notes, a bent teaspoon and a spring-knife with a bone handle. He, Valera and the surgeon surveyed this collection in silence.

"Identity card?"

"He didn't carry it, sir. I doubt if he ever had one."

"Are you from the village?"

"It's in my territory."

"Know anything about him?"

"Not a lot, sir. Everyone thought he was a bit of a weirdy. No relations anywhere, lived all by himself. A Red all right, we all knew that, but not the sort that has a clue as to what it's all about, not really. He didn't do any harm. I reckon after the Civil War he thought he was lucky to be still alive and played it careful."

"Not careful enough," said Valera. He picked up the spring-knife, flicked it open; tested the blade with the ball of his finger. "Funny that fellow didn't help himself to this. Probably thought he wouldn't need it. Probably thought he was God."

"You think it was this Moreno, sir?"

"Of course it was. Who else?" Valera put down the knife, picked up the medallion. St. Christopher, of course, with the Niño Jesu on his shoulder. "The silly old fool," he said. And turned away with his hands in his pockets, his shoulders hunched up high like a marabou stork's. "Now listen, sergeant. Somebody spoke to Andres. The morning before he died, perhaps, or the evening before. Somebody told him what message to give to Moreno. Moreno got the message all right; that's why he killed. You get back to that village as quick as you damned well can and find out just who it was that spoke to him. They probably came by car. Get the best description you can. Go through all the villages in the Alpujarra if you have to. Report to Captain Ostos before you go."

"*A la orden*," said the sergeant. He saluted, turned on his heel and left. The police surgeon lit a cigarette.

"He's got friends, then?"

"Who? Moreno?"

"Yes."

"Wolves hunt in a pack," said Valera tightly, "but they don't have friends. Nor has Moreno. He's a killer. He's a narcissist and a schizophrene and a manic depressive and a megalomane and anything else you bloody medicos want to call him, but first and foremost he's a killer. He hasn't got a friend in the world. He's a *killer*, you understand? Let's leave it at that."

The surgeon didn't reply, and Valera found himself at once regretting his outburst. It would be foolish, he thought, to let the responsibility for Moreno's release prey on one's nerves. The hunter must always be calm, cold-blooded. It was true that Moreno had no friends; but then . . . neither had he. . . .

"THE dog-whelk," said Professor Heinemann fondly. "Oh my, yes, the dog-whelk, *nucella lapillus*. Is one of the fiercest, the savagest killers of the sea. Oh yes indeed. I could tell you a story or two about Nucella." He caressed the lemon-yellow, curving shell with its intricate convolutions; returned it to one of his capacious pockets and instantly produced another. "*Mnja*. And this is Calliostoma. A fine specimen. Is perhaps the most beautiful of all, do you agree? A pity, almost, that he is not uncommon. Its beauty then would be appreciated more."

"Have another drink, Professor," said Sebastian Trout.

"Thank you, no. Is most kind of you, but I must be returning. *Aha*," said the Professor, producing yet another creature from some intimate recess of his person. "The periwinkle, yes, the *rough* periwinkle, *littorina rudis*. An interesting animal is this periwinkle. For instance, by no means is it commonly known that the male periwinkle possesses a penis."

"Ah," said Trout. "That explains it."

"Please?"

"I was wondering what a periwinkle would want to be rough about."

"Yah, yah," said the Professor vaguely. "That is so. Viviparous. Fertilisation takes place within the body of the female, and eggs through this rounded aperture will later emerge." He replaced Littorina in his pocket, began to fumble. "Now what have we next?"

Trout made a dive towards the bottle of Solera Fina on the table, poured himself out a nervous whack. "I can't take much more of this," he said, leaning perilously far forward and speaking in a whisper. "Where did you get *hold* of this dirty old man?"

"I didn't," said Fedora, opening one eye. "I don't know that I'd very much care to."

"A beautiful specimen, beautiful," hissed Trout savagely. "*Pedanticus hirsutus*, the Pomeranian waffler. Somebody ought to tell him that this gimmick went out with Conan Doyle."

"You tell him," said Fedora drowsily. A murderous glint entered Trout's eye. "My friend Fedora," he said vindictively. "Is one of the laziest, the inconsideratest bastards in Andalusia. Why should *I* be the one that has to. . . . What was that, Professor?" He bared his teeth in some approximation to an amicable grin and leaned back cautiously in his chair. The Professor caught him efficiently by the sleeve of his jacket and began to give him details of the singularly revolting love-life of *Balanus crenatus*, the acorn barnacle. Fedora closed his eye once again.

When he returned to consciousness some twenty minutes later, the Professor was nowhere in sight and the level of the wine in the bottle was some inches lower than formerly. Trout sat opposite him with his glass in his hand, staring between his knees at the ground and betraying all the symptoms of advanced alcoholic stupor. "Has he gone?" asked Fedora, sitting up.

"What?" said Trout, jumping. "Oh, it's you."

"Who did you think it was?"

"Oh, I don't know. I'm feeling a bit on edge if you want to know the truth. I'm going to *dream* about that old beanie tonight, I swear it."

"Might be an improvement, at that, from the sort of thing you usually seem to dream about. Has he gone?"

"Oh yes, he's gone. He said he wouldn't wake you up just to say goodbye, because," said Trout, a sadistic twist curling up the corner of his mouth, "he hopes to see us both again tomorrow."

"Funny how we're always meeting these peculiar types in the village. He's nothing like as bad as the General."

"My God, no," said Trout. "Don't talk to me about the General. Nearest thing I've ever seen to Gilles de Rais. Though if it comes to that, some of the things *that* old bird was saying just now were really a bit. . . . I mean, you wouldn't *think* it of barnacles, you honestly wouldn't. How anything so small and insignificant could be so utterly *depraved*."

"They have such lost, degraded souls, no wonder they inhabit holes."

"They don't," said Trout gloomily. "They don't. You're thinking of piddocks."

Fedora wasn't aware that he was thinking of anything in particular and was, on the whole, disposed to relish the state of mind that made such admirable abstraction possible. He sighed and leaned across towards the wine bottle. The body he thus extended was a shade under six feet in length, was spare, leggy and unostentatiously muscular, was terminated at one end by expensive blue suede shoes similar to those celebrated by Mr. Elvis Presley and others of that ilk and was gracefully concluded at the other by a thick mop of dark brown and mildly bewildered hair. The face directly beneath the hair was pleasant enough and attractively suntanned but was otherwise quite undistinguished, unless one happened to find the eyes—an impossibly light blue in tone and of a curious soft translucence—worthy of note. "Piddocks," he said, for no other reason than that the word struck him as euphonious and therefore deserving of repetition. He poured out the wine.

"You'd think," said Trout, "I could manage to pick up something better than that. Here we are just sitting at this bar all day, letting the talent float by. . . . Disgraceful, I call it."

"Well, it won't be as easy as you think. The word'll have got round by now."

"Word?" Trout looked belligerent. "What word?"

"I wouldn't want to sully my lips."

"Oh? So you wouldn't sully, cully? Well, it's all *your* fault if it's anyone's. Here I am, a quiet middle-aged gentleman of refined tastes, eking out my Civil Service pension in the pursuit of beauty and romance, traditional sanctity and loveliness—Sebastian Trout, the widows' friend—seeking peace and harmony, thinking tranquil, elevated thoughts—yes, but to hear *you* talk, anyone'd think I'd just broken out of a provincial tour of *The Summer of the Seventeenth Doll*. It's stinkers like you," said Trout, "make me want to crap."

"All right," said Fedora. "Spare us the Restoration dialogue." He wasn't really listening, however. He was buying an evening paper from the village newsboy. Trout watched him absently as he shook it open. "Anything hot?"

"I don't know yet. Let's see. Yes. Moreno's knocked off another."

"Where?"

"Some village or other up in the mountains."

"He's really cutting a rug, that bastard is," said Trout thoughtfully. "I'd hate to be a Spanish cop right now. I bet there's some poor sod who's having to change his trousers every five minutes while Slasher's on the loose."

"No need to be sordid," said Fedora, his voice partially muffled by the raised newspaper. After a pause, "Are the Foreign Office worried?"

"Worried? Hell, no. They're a thousand miles away. The people who have to worry are the people in the next street."

"There's something in that," said Fedora. He went on reading. In the end, he let the paper slide down on to his lap; put up a hand to run it through his already rumpled hair. "Just how good *was* he, Tiddler? In the war?"

"How good? He was the top. There was you and him and Palli and Nobby de Meyrignac, and all the others left at the post. Unless you count Otto Skorzeny, and he wasn't really in the same game, was he? Nobby died a few years back, or so they tell me, and you killed Gino Palli yourself that time in Trieste. So that leaves just you and Moreno. It's funny, really."

"Hilarious, isn't it? Or it would be, if he knew I was here."

"Thank God he doesn't," said Trout. "That's all *I* say."

"Why?"

"Because he's the sort of bastard who likes to think of himself as the one and only, that's why. He'd like to be the top man in his line of business, and it has to rile him a whole lot that he isn't ... *quite*."

"Good God," said Fedora. "He's welcome."

"He's a nasty piece of work. If you should ever run into him, don't look round for me. I'll be under the table."

"Well, but he must know that I've . . . sort of retired."

"In your game, you don't retire till they drag you off in a coffin. You know that as well as I do."

Fedora nodded. "You get bored," he said. "I've always heard that, and it's true. I'm beginning to wish Jimmy would get down to it and come across with *something* for us. I haven't had a job since last year in Amburu." He swung his feet out from under the table with a movement that, for him, was almost abrupt. "Know what I was thinking, Tiddler?"

"Yes. That it'd be simply crazy fun to join in the hunt."

". . . Something like that, maybe."

"Simply crazy is right. If someone was *paying* for it, it might be different. But helling round after Moreno just for the kicks, it's just not *mature*. You're incredible, you are," said Trout, shaking his head. "Adriana's only been away a fortnight, and here you are with surplus energy fairly fizzing out your earholes. We'd better go back to where we came in and find you some talent. Sex is more fun than anything, except making money."

Fedora yawned cavernously. "Right now I'm going home," he said. "I just don't like what I've heard about Moreno—that's all. Marbella's *my* parish, and he'd better not forget it."

"He doesn't even know it, "said Trout. "And it's just as well."

S PECIAL Operatives, whatever their age, sex or nationality, are usually inclined to be fatalistic. Their professional lives are spent, for the most part, in striving to carry out weird and unlikely assignments which, in the absence of definite information, they must assume to form part of a Great Design shaped by the statesmen and governing bodies of their respective countries. Before long, however, they notice that the success or failure of their individual missions has singularly little effect on the Great Design as such, which seems to pursue its own wobbly and erratic course quite independently of all external circumstance. Thus a Special Operative may have spent several months and a considerable sum of money in securing the blueprints of a new patent bottle-washer, only to find on his return that as a result of secret trade plans engineered by another department the machine in question is being manufactured under license in his own country and is available at any of the big chain stores for the price of two shillings and elevenpence. A very few such experiences serve to convince the Special Operative that he, more than other men, must regard himself as the plaything of an inscrutable providence, of an Imminent Will that dispenses O.B.E.'s and bullets in the belly with a grand unconcern. Experienced Special Operatives are Augustinians to a man. The suggestion that success in any field may be the reward of industry and merit rather than of the spin of an invisible and omnipotent roulette wheel will bring forth in them the sardonic smile, if not the sinister chuckle. Fedora and Feramontov saw eye to eye on remarkably few matters, but on this they were as one.

An O.B.E., of course, is a pleasant thing to have. Trout had been awarded his in 1946. But Adriana was something else again. Adriana was twenty-four. She was principal shareholder and executive director of the Jaguar S.A., an Argentine mining company believed to be tilting the scales at a round two hundred million dollars or so; she was intelligent, passionate, vindictive, charming, impulsive, cool-headed and tough as a root. She liked driving at a speed of a hundred and fifty, or as near to that as might be found convenient. Sometimes, however, she walked, and when she did so invariably left behind her a trail of semi-dislocated necks; crossing the Gran Via in Madrid just above the Plaza Callao, she once caused three cars to drive straight into one another and a heavy lorry to wrap itself round the traffic-lights. Her dressmaker was Balenciaga; not that that had anything to do with it.

And that, thought Trout, twisting his brown and near-naked body into a more comfortable position on the deckchair, *that* has gone and hooked on to old Johnny. Inexplicable, absolutely inexplicable. Of course, Johnny was an amusing enough fellow in his way, and reasonably good-looking in a dull light. But having said that, you'd said everything. Why, to do Fedora justice, he seemed as much surprised by it all as anybody. Perplexed, that was the word. Maybe his being a killer had something to do with it. If you've shot enough people in circumstances of indescribable sordidity, the

women seem to wait only for you to look at them before
they faint in your arms. According, at any rate, to the
writers of that branch of American fiction to which
Trout was most addicted. But there might be something
in it, all the same. Trout himself had killed a few people
in his time, but it wasn't the same and he knew it. He
didn't *look* like a killer. And Fedora did. Fedora had
death in his eyes. You had to know how to look for it,
yes, but a certain kind of woman knew by instinct. And
maybe Adriana was that kind of woman, down underneath. Um. Trout raised his left foot from the hot tiles.
Scratched his big toe.

Odd, all the same. Sticking to old Johnny, when she
had hundreds of really virile, handsome, muscular,
bronzed young men to choose from. Such as Trout
himself, for instance. Ah, well. She wouldn't be back
for at least another three weeks; that gave him a chance
to look around in the meantime. *Then* she would see
what an opportunity she'd missed. Besides, he was
getting a bit tired of playing gooseberry. Two's company, three's none.

. . . Though if one *had* to play gooseberry, one could
hardly hope to do it in more pleasant surroundings.
These South Americans knew more than you might
suppose about creature comforts. It had taken Adriana
two months to do the old place up, two months and he
hated to think how much money, but the results were
certainly tremendous. She'd picked a nice spot, to start
with. Two miles from the village on the Algeciras road,
between the sea and the mountains, where a high
buttress of land gave shelter from the wind and incidentally a magnificent view across the whole of the
Straits of Gibraltar as far as Africa. There were palm

trees and umbrella pines to mingle their scents and to
offer shade from the sun; behind the clipped privet of
the hedges there was mimosa and bougainvillea, gar-
denias and *damas de noche*. Steps led down from the
pergola to the sea, where there was soft sand and a good
bathing beach; farther to the right was a tiled swimming-pool with a high diving-board, a changing room
and an enormous refrigerator with about five years'
supply of Munich beer stacked away inside it. The
house itself had been remodelled by an Italian architect
the preceding winter, and was now an opulent dream
of pastel-shaded walls, cool cream-coloured floors,
ultra-modern furniture and gigantic nickel-plated bath-
rooms in which a carelessly-touched switch might
produce a shower of needle-cold water, a fluffy hygienic
face-towel, a vibro-massage, an electric razor or the
Vienna Philharmonic Orchestra playing Beethoven's
Ninth. Trout preferred, on the whole, the simpler
amenities offered by the swimming-pool and the
refrigerator. And, of course, by the Mediterranean sun,
now rising above the level of the palmtops, whose
beneficial rays he could absorb quite as pleasantly there
as anywhere else.

It was getting late, though; there was the inner, as
well as the outer, Trout to be considered. He tilted his
wrist, looked at his watch. Yes, five past ten. Time for
breakfast. He put on his jazzy green-and-violet beach
shirt; examined the bottles on the table at his side and,
having successfully detached the only remaining full
one from the three dead soldiers beside it, downed its
contents in a couple of gulps. He then picked up from
the ground at his feet his Ronson, his tooled leather
cigarette-case, his pigskin wallet and his copy of *Guilty*

Detective Stories. His sunglasses were on the table; he put them on. His *alpagata* sandals were lying at the edge of the pergola. He put them on, too. Then, a shade blearily, he made his way up and along the verandah to the french windows that gave on to the sitting-room.

Johnny was there inside, planted lugubriously at the Bechstein grand and playing some beastly artificial-sounding muck by lousy old Bach. Trout put his head in through the window. "What about eats?"

"Whenever you like."

Trout entered; plodded importantly over to the table, seated himself and jammed down the buzzer which would, as past experience had taught him, bring about the miraculous appearance of Carmen, a small, neat and delectable maidservant, with the breakfast tray. Carmen really wasn't bad at all. Trout, who wasn't snobbish in such matters, might not have bothered to look farther if she hadn't been a local girl and equipped with a local *novio*, who, in his turn, was in all probability equipped with a local sheath-knife. As things were, Trout chose to content himself with giving her English lessons, instructing her in the more essential and elementary phrases relative to her profession. "What's for breakfast?" he asked, as she rustled into sight.

"Egg," she said. She put the tray down on the table.

"Egg? Good God. What's for afters?"

"Yes."

"What d'you mean, *yes*? Oh, all right, skip it. Bring me beer."

"Beer, yes."

"More beer. Lots of beer. Buckets of beer."

"Beer, yes." She nodded enthusiastically. That word,

at least, had sunk in by now. "Bring beer," she said. And, as an afterthought, giggled. She then retired gracefully as Fedora came mooching round the corner, tastefully dressed in blue denim jeans and a K.D. bush shirt. He sat down heavily opposite Trout, who had already picked up a spoon and was knocking chips off the top of the eggshell. "Where've you been?" he asked, with no great show of interest.

"Oh, swimming. Sunbathing. Loafing. Getting quite a decent tan, wouldn't you say? Now's the best time, before the sun gets too strong." Trout peered approvingly downwards at the yawning gap in his beach shirt above his navel. "You ought to come down there yourself, instead of bashing that blasted piano about all day long. It'd do you good."

"I go down there sometimes," said Fedora. "For target practice."

"Target practice?"

"That's right. With the Mauser. I've got a doofer that chucks plate things up in the air at irregular intervals. Adriana's idea, that was. I never seem to hit anything. It's depressing."

"Look, don't you *ever* relax?"

Fedora seemed to consider this question as unworthy of any reply. He was staring at the plate directly in front of him, favouring an innocent-looking boiled egg with what Adriana called his Highway Patrol Chief expression. "For God's sake," he said. "Do we *have* to have eggcups with gold rims round the top?"

"Oh, don't be such a creep. It's the proper thing. I mean, you can't be any old sort of secret agent these days, you got to have social catchit."

"I'm not a secret agent. I haven't been for years."

"That's not the point," said Trout severely. He lifted up his egg in his fingers, examined the eggcup cautiously. His expression changed. "My God, it *is* gold. *Real* gold. My God." He put the egg back, dug his spoon tentatively into it as though in search of fresh auriferous deposits. "I suppose it does for the holidays, when she's not inclined to be fussy."

"That's right," said Fedora glumly. "Don't try and put it in your pocket when you've finished. This isn't Maxim's."

Trout looked injured. Carmen reappeared, bearing toast on a salver and two open bottles of beer. "It worries me a bit." said Johnny, pushing his glass towards her. "It really does."

"What?"

"All this soft living. Maybe it's the climate as much as anything else. I wouldn't want to go all mushy."

Trout's mouth opened, as though in stupefaction. "You? Mushy? *You?*"

"Well, why not? It happens. You know it does."

"I know where all this comes from," said Trout, reaching for the toast. "What's this? Caviare? Whacko. No, it's this chap Moreno. As soon as a fellow in your own line of business hops out of jail and opens up shop with two or three nice juicy knifings, damned if you don't start absolutely champing at the bit. Harry Hotspur's nothing to it. If that's the way you really feel about things, you ought to go and work for the Russians. They're about the only people nowadays who seem to have a war on, even if nobody else knows about it."

"We did get an offer from the Chinese once, didn't we? Remember old Colonel Yang? My word. What a blister."

"Maybe you should have taken him up."

"Well . . . it might have been interesting," said Fedora; so thoughtfully that Trout lowered the piece of toast he was munching and stared at him in horror.

"You don't mean you'd work for the other side, Johnny? You couldn't do *that*."

"Oh, I don't know."

Trout resumed his munching. "It *would* be a lark, at that. Jesus, they'd do their collective nut up at Whitehall, if you did. Burgess and Maclean'd look like last month's dirty washing. They'd probably even send someone out to *get* you. . . . Only trouble is, it might be me."

"Hell, no. You'd come too."

"Oh, no, I wouldn't."

Fedora shrugged. "Anyway," he said, "the real reason why I won't do it is because it's quite on the cards that nobody'd take the slightest notice at all. And that'd be too damned dispiriting for words. And there again, no one's asked me." He pushed back his chair. "Coming into the village?"

"What for?"

"The mail."

"Oh well. All right."

THEY drove into the village and parked, as usual, opposite the Sandua bar. A dozen or so assorted tourists were seated, as usual, at the pavement tables under the red-and-white awning. "*Ow*," said Trout suddenly. He'd bitten his tongue.

"What's the matter?"

"There's the Per . . . the Professor."

"Oh Lord. Let's get out of here."

Trout had one hand clapped over his mouth; peculiar mumblings emerged. "Yes," he said, removing it, "but *look*."

Fedora turned his head and looked. The Professor was there, sure enough, sitting at the nearest of the tables; and next to him, behind a long glass of gin-and-limejuice, was a darkhaired girl in a neat white Irish linen costume. Her long brown legs were visible under the table, and a small group of local layabouts were standing at some ten yards' distance, commenting upon them in almost-audible undertones. "Bread on the waters," said Trout reverentially. "That's what it is, bread on the waters. Where d'you suppose the old devil picked up a humdinger like *that* one?"

"I don't know," said Johnny. "We could always ask."

"Yes. We could. Let's."

They got out of the car and commenced a circumpect approach. The girl—who was listening, chin in hand, to the Professor, and with every outward sign of respectful attention—looked up at them as they reached the table. "Good morning, Professor," said Trout heartily, contriving to sound like a Rugby footballer just down from Trinity. "A beautiful, beautiful morning. Yes, indeed."

"Ah," said the Professor. "It is you."

"And may we join you?"

"Delighted. Delighted." The Professor, having overcome his initial difficulty in focusing upon them, indeed seemed to be actually pleased to see them, in a jovial, muddle-headed way; it was even possible, thought Fedora, that he remembered who they were. "Yes, yes, please sit down. We do not observe the formalities. You will join us in a glass of wine?"

"We should like that above all things," said Trout oozily, hitching his chair in to the table.

"You do not know, I think, my good friend and assistant, Miss Weber? Miss Weber is with our expedition. She is a marine biologist."

"Oh, I say, not really?" said Trout, sounding more than ever like something out of P. G. Wodehouse. "Marine biology, eh? Slashin' trade, that." He leaned forward enthusiastically. "My name is Trout — Sebastian Trout—and this is Johnny Fedora."

Miss Weber, who was returning her glass rather hurriedly to the table in order to take Trout's proferred hand, released it a fraction too early and it tilted over. "Bu . . . Dash it," said Trout, recovering simultaneously his balance and his equanimity. "No, no, please, it doesn't matter. Good for the material, actually." He brushed frantically at the knees of his trousers, shooting a fine alcoholic spray towards the neighbouring tables.

"I am so *sorry*," said Miss Weber. "It was so clumsy of me, do please forgive me."

She produced a large man's handkerchief from the white handbag on the table; Trout accepted it gratefully and, with it, managed soon to mop up the worst of the damage. "Quite all right," he said. "Don't suppose it stains, what? I mean, what was it?"

"A gin and lime. No, I don't think it will stain."

"Hang on a jiffy, I'll order you another."

Fedora was, on the whole, content to sit back and watch. It was a long time since he had seen anyone even remotely as physically attractive as Adriana, nor was he now ready to admit that this Miss Weber might be, in that respect alone, Adriana's equal; loyalty apart, however, Fedora's eyesight was as excellent as ever and undeniably, looking at Miss Weber might well be counted among life's more pleasant and agreeable experiences. In a way, her beauty was a complement to Adriana's; she was tall and slim and leggy like a colt where Adriana was . . . how to put it? . . . pneumatic; she had jet-black hair where Adriana's was uncompromisingly and flamingly red; the tan of her skin would have offset perfectly Adriana's pearl-smooth paleness. It would be interesting, Fedora thought, to see them both together, so as to. . . . Or no, maybe it wouldn't. Things perhaps were better as they were. The combination of red hair and Argentine blood makes for a highly explosive mixture, and Fedora chose to take no unnecessary chances.

"Trout?" the Professor was saying. "Your name is Trout, yes? Is interesting. *Forelle*, we say in German. I have some very fine trouts, in fact, in my little aquarium near Hanover. I have examined the pigmentation. The surface-swimming predators have the underparts frequently colourless, as you will know, and this in order with the surface film of the water to blend that the beast be thus invisible to enemies in the deeps. Is true of penguins, even, and of water-shrews. I think my researches will in part this strange problem elucidate, if problem so it is that has this natural explanation. I have examined the pigmentation of the eye in a large number of trouts and I find there exists a relationship. . . . "

He went on and on, his heavy beard twitching with excitement, the wine in the glass he held bobbing crazily from side to side. There could be no denying his enthusiasm, thought Fedora; a bleak look-out for Tiddler if the girl suffered from the same kind of virus. Obviously she did, to some extent, or she couldn't possibly have put up with the Professor day in and day out. That was if she really *was* his assistant and not the other thing. She certainly didn't look very scientific. But then not all of them did.

What a thing to be mad about, though. Fish. Obviously Tiddler would get off to the hell of a good start with her, with a name like his. *Mrs. Trout, marine biologist.* That would be a bit too good to be true.

Fedora sat back, folded his hands on his lap. *A good start,* he was thinking; exactly what the name *had* given her. She'd knocked her glass over. Except that it hadn't been Trout's name. It had been his own. Of course, accidents did happen; that went without saying. But then why was he now feeling so suddenly, so inexplicably alert? Could she *really* be that?

A bit too good to be true?

I T was the first time that Elsa had seen Feramontov completely furious and, moreover, not bothering to conceal it. "There will, of course, be hell to pay for this. I'll see to it personally. I'll have someone's guts hanging from the clothes-line before this dam' business is over." He drummed with his fingers on the tabletop. "A complete and utter failure where we can't afford failures at all. I'll have to see Bruniev about it, I've got no alternative. I'll take a taxi into Malaga this afternoon."

"It changes the situation?"

"Of course it does. Radically. We hadn't allowed for British Intelligence, because we'd no reason to suppose they were even interested. Result, they plank two operatives down to wait for us and as near as a toucher we walk straight into the trap. All I can say is that their information service has to be about six times better than ours, and I'm just not prepared to work under those conditions. Damn it, it *scares* me."

"The thing I don't understand is that those two men have been there for *weeks*. We didn't get orders ourselves—"

"I know, I know. That's *it*. It's a leakage. A top level leakage. And it's too late to do a thing about it. We have to push on as planned, we haven't any choice. And of all the people it could have been. . . . " His voice died slowly away, returned disconcertingly at full strength.

". . . It has to be Trout and Fedora. *Fedora*. I mean, it's
Moreno they're after, it sticks out a mile."

"Their cover story is so good," said Elsa hesitantly,
"I was almost beginning to wonder if it mightn't be
sheer coincidence. I mean, he *is* Adriana Tocino's boy
friend. It got into the papers, if you remember. It
doesn't seem—"

"Well, I can't deny that one comes across the most
amazing tricks of fate in this line of business—and all
the time. But I'm just not prepared to accept it. In just
the same way as he probably won't accept your having
spilt that glass over the table. You'll have to watch
those nerves of yours, Elsa, you really will."

She made a helpless gesture with her hands. "It gave
me a shock when he said it right out like that. You'd
think at least he'd use a . . . a *nom-de-guerre*. If he'd said
anything else, we'd never have suspected."

"And that's the thing I like least of all. He must have
done it just to test your reactions, and that must mean
they'd suspected the Professor already, I can't imagine
why. When you spilt that bloody glass, you may have
given the whole dam' game away."

"Well, I'm sorry. I'm very sorry."

"It's hardly enough to be sorry, is it?" said Feramontov; and hit her, unexpectedly and very hard, with
the back of his hand. Her hair jolted back with the
blow, and her fingers dug suddenly into the deep foam-
rubber arms of her chair; stayed there while she stared
at him, while the red flush of the impact died slowly out
along her left cheekbone. "It doesn't help, you know,"
she said, almost with contempt. "It doesn't help at all."

"It relieves my feelings," said Feramontov, already
moving away from her. He placed his hands on the

table and leaned heavily over it, his head bowed down as though awaiting the axe. "You say they're coming here?"

"In an hour's time or so. The Professor invited them ... naturally, just the way we'd agreed. I couldn't find any way to tip him off."

"It doesn't matter. We have to continue with the plan, because we've got no option. I'm going to Malaga, as I said; I'll be out of the way. Moreno had better stay below decks while they're here. I'll tell him." He turned his head round sharply. "Above all, don't let *him* know. About Fedora."

"I've never met anybody quite like those two before," said Elsa, saying for once exactly what she felt and regardless of its relevance. After all, she had *seen* Fedora; a pleasant-faced man with nice hands and with eyes that crinkled at the corners in the sunlight. Only a certain alertness, a certain aura of dangerousness to indicate that he was anything at all out of the usual. Fedora had no *business*, she felt, to look like that. And as for Trout. . . .

"How do you mean?"

"Well ... Fedora ... There's no sort of ... of *urgency* about him, you know what I mean? Is he really as good as they say he is?"

Feramontov turned, resting the back of his thighs against the table. "You haven't much experience, have you, Elsa, of people on the other side?"

"Not much. No."

"They have quite a few people rather like Fedora. And you sum them up rather well when you say that there's no sense of urgency about them. They seem to lack a spirit of dedication. In a word, seriousness.

They're not like *us*. And they certainly aren't like Moreno. All I can tell you is that appearances are deceptive and that many of those people are very good indeed, though perhaps no one of them is quite as good as Fedora. Fedora doesn't kill because he likes it, or even because he's an idealist. He kills the way other people kill mosquitoes . . . absent-mindedly, as it were . . . in a kind of self-defence, preventing anyone else from getting bitten. He doesn't *blame* the mosquito for wanting to bite, you see; he doesn't get worked up about it at all, the way some of our people do. And that means he comes as near as anyone to having no weaknesses whatsoever."

"He has one."

"What's that?"

"He likes women. I'm sure of it."

Feramontov smiled, though a trifle tiredly. "Whenever I hear a woman say that of anyone, I know that she thinks that he's been attracted to *her*. In the majority of cases, it's pure wishful thinking; but in this case, it conceivably mightn't be. The fact that he guesses you're a Communist agent would add immensely to your attraction. One of the most hackneyed themes of popular Western fiction is that of the beautiful Russian who falls for, as they say, some bronzed and rugged symbol of the capitalist countries. Before the beautiful Russian, it was the kind-hearted prostitute; the principle of a satisfying redemption remained the same. Were you thinking, Elsa, of reversing this process and converting Fedora to the joys of genuine democracy?"

"I wouldn't mind trying. He looks like more of a man than most people I've met, and there's not much wrong with the other fellow's build, either . . . if it comes to *that*."

"I don't think it will come to that," said Feramontov. He took two quick steps to stand in front of her, leaned forward to speak with greater deliberation. "In the first place, our present expedition has no room for proselytes. In the second place, I've no reason to think that Bruniev would trust you sufficiently. You lack experience, Elsa. That is always unfortunate, and it has been known to be fatal. Do you understand me?"

"Yes. I think so."

"*I* have experience. And so I know that those stupid books have an element of truth. The men on the other side are *always* attractive—that was what Juliet liked about Romeo. And look what happened to *her*. She was stupid, too; a stupid girl in what is really a very stupid play, though the poetry I grant is not without merit. Don't confuse literature and life, Elsa. That's a typically bourgeois failing."

Elsa looked contemplative. She was thinking, in fact, of the library in the University of Moscow, with the collected works of Vilyami Shekspira, edited by Vengerov, bound in brown leather on the middle shelves; she thought of the wide shuffling silence, of the paper-strewn tables, and was conscious of something that she might have thought was nostalgia, had not that also been stigmatised as a hopelessly bourgeois attitude. She had never thought Juliet particularly stupid, oddly enough. *She doth teach the torches to shine bright.* . . . Elsa felt suddenly and strangely lost, as though Moscow and Vilyami Shekspira had never been so far away from her. That was, of course, literally true. But all the same. . . . She spoke to Feramontov, trying to keep this new sense of desolation from her voice.

"What about tonight? You said there'd be no time for a change of plan."

"Nor there is. No, tonight you can exert all the charm you wish upon them. You can even," said Feramontov querulously, "revert for a while to the role of the good-hearted prostitute. If by some means or other we can succeed in keeping those two stuck here while Moreno gets on with the job, we've every chance of pulling the whole thing off successfully. Meanwhile, I'll have to get moving. They ought to be along here any minute."

THE three men drove down to the village harbour together, all three jammed tight in the front seat of the Sunbeam Alpine; Trout at the wheel, Johnny to the left, and Professor Heinemann in the middle, with his whiskery features pushed forward between the two of them like the target of an Aunt Sally in a fun fair. He talked learnedly and interminably on the topic of What Makes Limpets Stick, while Trout and Fedora listened in optimistic silence. Eventually Trout brought the car to a halt on the weathered cement of the harbour mole and, one by one, they clambered out, the Professor still gassing away about adductor and depresser muscles, opercular and scutal plates. It was, as Trout had already remarked, a beautiful morning. Just sufficient breeze was blowing in from the sea to alleviate the full weight of the Spanish sun and to tip with white flecks the waves beyond the harbour wall; within the harbour itself, however, the water was smooth as glass and surprisingly clear. At the landward end of the mole were grouped a cluster of single-storey fisherman's cottages, glaring white against the red-brown earth behind them, and a half-dozen blue-clad Spaniards, diminished by distance to Lilliputian size, sat beside the houses mending their nets. To the north-west and far in the background the mountains rose towards the sky, a clean crystalline grey, their sheer slopes spiderwebbed with fissures that cast deep, fantastic shadows down their flanks. The air smelt of salt, of olive oil and of rusty iron.

"Is that the boat?" asked Trout, breaking dexterously into a pause in Heinemann's monologue. The Professor blinked, followed the direction of Trout's pointing finger as though uncertain as to what the devil he could be referring. "Yes," he said. "Oh yes. That's the boat."

Since the only other vessels in sight were fishermen's dinghies, this had seemed fairly obvious from the first. The yacht lay moored at the foot of the steps a little to their left, a smart, rakish job resplendent with fresh white paint and polished brass; it suggested the lazy frivolities of Hellenic cruises and junketings off Capri rather than the ardours of scientific exploration, but it went well enough with Elsa Weber. "Polarlys," said Trout, reading the name on the stern. "Very pretty."

"Pretty, yes. She is a very fine boat, we are lucky to have her. It is through this kind generosity of the owner, our French benefactor whose name I mention to you, *denke ich*. One Pierre Cazamian. A charming, pleasant fellow. *Ungekunstelt*, if you understand me, but a pleasant fellow and stinking rich."

Elsa suddenly appeared on deck, dressed rather startlingly though discreetly enough in a yellow one-piece swimsuit. "Come on aboard," she said, beckoning. She was probably accustomed to taking the lead in this way whenever her respected chief's ditherings grew too protracted. "This way, please."

She sounded rather like the brighter kind of air hostess, reflected Johnny as he walked down the steps. Health and Efficiency. Strength through Joy. All very Aryan. The usual outward imperturbability; in all likelihood, the usual devastating lack of any sense of humour. He mounted the posh grey gangplank with the highly-polished handrail and paused for a moment on deck, wondering where the fo'c'sle was and if he ought not to salute it. There seemed to be nobody about. "Here we are, here we are," said the Professor, arriving beside him and pawing at the deck in his eagerness like a bull about to charge. "You will wish to see the laboratory, yes, the specimens, the equipment. Elsa will show you all. Elsa, you have the key to the laboratory?"

"The key will be in the usual place, Herr Professor."

"Then take our visitors down to show them our experiments. You will explain them everything. While I must the new report from Hettering examine."

"This way, please," said Elsa, dimpling.

Trout and Fedora followed her long brown legs through the frosted-glass door and down a carpeted corridor. She stopped outside a green door about half-way down the passage, took a key from a hook placed to one side of a projection in the bulkhead, and opened the door without apparent effort. Fedora, who knew how keys tend to stick in the salt-laden atmosphere aboard a yacht, admired the organisation that allowed for a weekly drop of oil on unimportant hinges; not all scientific expeditions are run with scientific precision, but this one seemed to be. "What," he asked, "exactly is it all in aid of?"

"Please?" said Elsa, pausing with the door half-open.

"Just what is the *aim* of this expedition?"

"Oh, *that*. It is all to do with dear little baby jelly-fish."

"I never knew jellyfish *had* babies. The rough periwinkle, of course—"

"I was joking, in part. No—it seems that last summer

they had an invasion of jellyfish all along this coast, and the tourist people here got fed up with it. It puts off many people from coming, obviously, if you can't have a bathe without getting stung by a lot of jellyfish. So the Ministerio de Turismo asked the Herr Professor if he could do something about it."

"I see," said Johnny. "And can he?"

"That remains to be seen. Come on in."

Trout and Fedora stepped through the open door into the cabin. It certainly wasn't large, but it was large enough to contain a full-size thirty-three-inch high bench loaded with an impressive assortment of clamps, plastic receptacles, rubber tubes, glass beakers and with what looked like a miniature model of a form-fit transformer. There were deep steel lockers to either side of what looked like an ordinary Westinghouse refrigerator, and—against the near wall—a couple of comfortable armchairs. "Oh, very nice," said Trout. "What's it do?"

"Most of the equipment you see on the bench is used to analyse ordinary sea-water. We collect samples from various places and from various depths. We note the temperature, we test the salinity, we examine the organic matter it contains. Then we analyse it chemically. The results we enter into a lodger."

"A ledger."

"What? Yes, a ledger. Other samples we preserve at different temperatures and we keep ephyrae in them." She tapped the test-tube rack with the tip of one finger. "Medusae, you see. Little baby jellyfish. Look closely and you will see them. Well, and from all this we discover what sort of seawater these jellyfish like the best."

"We know that already," objected Trout. "They like it here."

"Well, they *arrive* here. They follow the currents of the water that they like. And when we know just what kind of water that is, we too can follow the currents, but in reverse. And so find the colonies where they breed. Because these very little jellyfish are formed from parent hydroids which do not swim at all—they're fixed. In rock pools, in reefs, and so on. We find where the hydroids live, we destroy them, no more jellyfish." She smiled ravishingly at Trout. "All very simple."

Fedora, meanwhile, had gone round behind the bench and was staring down into the three-feet-square metal tank on the far side. Beneath its plate-glass cover was a festering mass of jellyfish, orange, greeny-white and brown, hideous toadstool-like shapes writhing aimlessly to and fro, their tentacles trailing beneath them like strips of macerated flesh. "This is where you keep the big ones?"

"Yes. Chrysaora, mostly. Those are larger than usual, of course, because they have grown under perfect conditions. I find the colouring very pretty, myself."

"Yes, beautiful," said Trout, cautiously retreating a couple of paces. "And I wouldn't want them any bigger than they are. Do they sting?"

"Most certainly they do."

She leaned forward to peer down into the submersion tank, chewing her underlip thoughtfully. "Craziest damned thing I ever saw," said Trout to Johnny, in an undertone. "Freudian-looking objects, aren't they? Reminds me of the Queen of Sheba and her pet amoeba —we ought to try the Professor with *that* one."

"What did it do? The amoeba?"

"It tenderly murmured, *Ich liebe*. Very appropriate, you see. At any rate, up to the end of the first verse. The later stanzas aren't quite so Teutonic, d'you mean to say you don't *know* it?"

"You forget I wasn't educated in a public school."

". . . I think," said Elsa, turning back towards them rather abruptly, "I will now show you our diving equipment. That'll interest you more, won't it? It isn't science, after all, so much as sport."

"Sport, eh?" said Trout enthusiastically, back-pedalling to let her move past him. "Bang on. We definitely care for that."

They went back into the corridor. Elsa locked the door carefully behind her, then led the way towards the foredeck; stopping outside a white-painted door on the port side bearing the stencilled inscription, ALMACEN. It wasn't locked. The room behind it was smaller than the other; most of the available space within was taken up by stacks of compressed-air cylinders; on the shelves to the right were a half-dozen or so rubber diving masks, and hanging from hooks on the walls was a varied selection of harpoon-guns, hand-nets and barbed spears of a sufficiently murderous appearance. "Sport," said Trout, "I thought you said? Looks more like the tribal arsenal of the Chippeway Indians."

"Here we keep our diving gear," said Elsa, ignoring him. "Aqualungs and so forth. Nowadays we study marine biology in the field as much as we can, just as other naturalists do. This equipment makes it possible. Here you see the case for the underwater camera. Very important and very expensive, I'm afraid. The Klieg lights we use are stored on the rack above. They are very powerful. They have to be. These tubes contain compressed air. A diver normally carries two of them and each one lasts about an hour. In fact we hardly ever dive for more than forty-five minutes. Longer is sometimes dangerous, psychologically speaking. Have you ever done any diving, Mr. Fedora?"

"I've been down once or twice," said Johnny. "That was in England, though. I had a frogman's suit."

"A *frogman*, yes, that's what you call it. Well, but here we work at quite shallow depths and the water is warm, especially in the summer, so we don't need special suits. I usually wear a bikini."

"Ah," said Trout. "*Now* we see what you meant."

"*These* are geological hammers," said Elsa, picking one up purposefully. "Hammers and chisels, for taking rock samples. We label them and keep them in specimen cases for classification later. These are tape measures. Accurate measurements are very important, Mr. Trout, particularly when one wears a bikini. Mine are 36-23-35. I can therefore wear a two-foot belt, like this one; you load them with lead weights according to the depth you expect to be swimming at. *Yours* would need to be about three foot six, I imagine."

"Oh here! I say!" said Trout.

"Under water, you can check your depth with this instrument which you strap to your wrist like a watch. It measures the hydrostatic pressure. We also have photo-electric instruments for measuring the amount of light reaching any given surface. Very sensitive, of course, for undersea work. Our equipment is really very complete. In the far corner is the high explosive."

"High explosive?" said Trout, startled. "Where?"

"Plastic eight-oh-eight. It's quite safe, it won't go off unless it's detonated. We use it to clear superficial sand from a rocky surface, or to break up rock specimens, and sometimes to kill all the fish within a given area so that we can check on them statistically. Fish are very sensitive to vibrations, and you can kill an awful lot of them with a very little H.E. You'd be surprised."

"I am," said Trout. "I am. And the, er, harpoons?"

"For single specimens. We don't use them a lot, though. The main advantage of the aqualung equipment is that it enables us to study the living animals in their natural habitat. Once they are dead, they're laboratory cases." She shrugged. "Of course, there's plenty of work to be done in the laboratory still. Dissection, analysis of organs, classification. But field study is much more interesting. It's very beautiful, down there in the water. If you've only tried it in the north you'll have no idea how clear the Mediterranean can be. We could dive now for a few minutes, if you liked."

Fedora was in fact already trying on one of the masks. It seemed to fit him snugly enough; a circle of stiff rubber that moulded itself to his forehead, cheeks and upper lip with a six-inch oval of mica before his eyes, giving him a wider field of vision than he had expected. "We haven't any swimming trunks," he said regretfully.

"Oh, I can lend you some. Not mine, of course. Mine wouldn't fit. But we have some spares."

Johnny pulled off the visor, looked at Trout. "What do you think? Care for a dip?"

"I rather think so," said Trout. "Sounds more fun than analysing organs."

MALAGA was sweltering in the morning sunshine. The street outside the office was deserted. When the bald man reached to lower the blind, the little room was instantly tinged with greenish light like the inside of a grotto or of a tank in an aquarium. Feramontov was instantly reminded of the specimen tank aboard the *Polarlys*; Bruniev's great hairless dome, swimming uncertainly to and fro in the sudden dimness, certainly bore a resemblance to the bell of a jellyfish. The idea was fanciful, though; Feramontov abandoned it at once.

"If I'm not mistaken," he said, as the other man sat down at the desk and began to leaf abstractedly through the folders there, "Fedora is what on our side we should call a liquidator. And a good one."

"A good one," said Bruniev, "and a lucky one. Yes."

"But just how lucky?"

"I've got the report here," said Bruniev, his shiny head lowered now over the papers. "It seems he started off with the Special Operations Executive when he was barely twenty years old. And this is the liquidation list. Gailland, the collaborationist. Hartmann of the Gestapo. Kreisler, who was on the *Lagenunabhangige* torpedo project, and Mohr who was on the V.2's. Busch and Schnee, just when they thought they'd got the answer to the British microwave radar. Kiefer of the Gestapo. Those are all definite. There's a dozen more 'attributed'. Then after the war, he broke up neo-Nazi groups running in England and Paris, he killed Karl Mayer in Austria and Panagos in Trieste, and he spoilt one of *our* little efforts when he shot Gino Palli. He killed Per Gunnar Holmgren up in Sweden while our agents were still dithering about in Venice, and he's thought to have had a hand in that funny business last year down in Argentina. All in all, he'd make for quite a nasty problem if his removal was ever considered necessary. Even for someone like Moreno. As it is," he said, closing the folder with a little flip, "I'm not convinced that it *is* necessary, or even advisable."

"You can't believe that he's there in Marbella purely through coincidence?"

Bruniev lifted his hands into the air like a Spaniard— a gesture so conscientiously rehearsed as to seem altogether natural. "Coincidences happen. All our agents' reports seem to indicate that he's there by chance. I don't feel that Head Office would accept any change of plan *because* he's there. It's just an incidental hazard like any other."

"I'm sorry you take that point of view."

"What point of view do you expect me to take? You have your instructions and I have no authority to rescind them. Quite the reverse."

Feramontov nodded. "But you have the authority to delegate me a few expert assistants, should I decide them to be necessary."

"On a liquidation project?"

"That's what we were talking about, wasn't it?"

"Yes, but. . . . Yes. I have."

"Good. That was the point I wished to clarify. You'll realise that we can't involve Moreno in the

matter; he's far too valuable. Except possibly. . . . "
Feramontov allowed the corners of his mouth to turn
briefly upwards in something not very like a smile.
"Elsa is at this moment persuading them to take up
skin-diving. Elsa can be very persuasive, when she
chooses. And at fifteen or twenty fathoms' depth,
accidents have been known to happen to inexperienced
divers."

"You like to slant the odds."

"Naturally. That's common sense. Fedora may be up
to Moreno's weight on land," said Feramontov,
stretching himself luxuriously, "but I doubt if he'll be
as good in the water. *Or* as lucky. Thirty feet down—
that's where we want him."

"Thirty feet down," said Bruniev dubiously. "I
see. . . . "

. . . But Fedora, in a mild way, was enjoying himself.

He was absolutely alone. He was as though tucked
away inside a tiny glass-fronted case; he was inside the
glass, everything else was outside. Everything, including
his own body. His hands, appearing from time to time
a foot or so in front of his face, no longer seemed to
belong to him; they were strange inanimate objects
whose movements were somehow co-related to his own
muscular contractions. Elsa was swimming a couple of
yards to his left and slightly lower, Trout rather farther
to his right; neither of them mattered; they had nothing
to do with him, nothing whatsoever. Fedora was a pair
of eyes and a brain behind a vaseline-smeared plastic
panel; human beings no longer had any connection
with him, because he was no longer human. He was

disembodied spirit. He was something between a bird, a space traveller and a fish.

At first, swimming on the surface and watching the smoothly wrinkled sands move by some twenty feet beneath him, he had felt a powerful and unpleasant sense of vertigo; but once they had all three tucked down their heads and dived to the harbour floor, his unease had disappeared and he had become—in a paradoxical way—at home. The lead weights in his belt no longer tugged him downwards, his stomach no longer felt as though it might at any moment be sucked down and away from him in an invisible spiralling vortex. He was, in fact, no longer conscious of weight at all.

Experiment showed that he could roll over on to his back, sit on the water with his feet just clear of the sand at the bottom, spin himself round and round like a diving aeroplane—all without the slightest difficulty or discomfort. It wasn't tiring. It was relaxing, if anything. And Elsa had been right about the beauty of the sea bottom. Fedora, as it happened, was normally unappreciative of natural beauty, but the world of the sea bed fascinated him—perhaps because its beauty wasn't natural at all; it was *un*-natural, fantastic.

Looking up, he could see the sunlight broken by the wavelets on the surface into shuddering, boiling bands and flecks, into streamers of bright gold and orange that became suddenly alive with all the colours of the prism; and he could see the bubbles of his own breath rising swiftly, colourless like pearls, then glinting as though with flame as they reached that surface froth, mingled with it and disappeared. Around him he could see fish, fish like grey ghosts, fleeing and twisting through the

dim depths of the harbour; a whole shoal glinting like
a shower of silver daggers as they turned together away
from the approaching swimmers. The sea bed there
was of fine white sand, almost free of seaweed, but on
isolated clusters of rock he saw an occasional blaze of
writhing colour, of red and blue laminaria fronded like
palm leaves and moving in the undercurrents as in a
slow, strong wind. On the sand itself, small crabs
scuttled to and fro, vanishing as his shadow loomed
over them, and ugly, tiny fishes like blennies with great
staring eyes burrowed deep down and out of sight. He
saw no big fish, nothing of more than a foot in length,
but he hadn't expected to. No jellyfish either, thank
goodness. If any were about, they would be higher up,
near the surface.

Elsa led them round the harbour in a slow, swinging
circle until they came up against the wall; they turned
then to follow it round to where the yacht lay moored.
Fedora was aware, in that strange dissociated way, of
the general direction they were taking as he was aware
of Elsa's movements to his left; sometimes she was close,
almost brushing his elbow, at other times shooting
casually forward like a torpedo with a few quick stabs
of her blue flippers, pivoting in mid-flight to flash down
to sand level and to dig her outstretched fingers into the
soft sea floor. She was seeing numberless things that he
was missing, but then she knew exactly what to look for.
This was like the African jungle that Fedora knew so
well; underwater, one had to learn to use one's eyes all
over again. Like the Congo, but not so dangerous, of
course. Or was it? . . .

She showed him one of her captures before slipping it
into the fine-mesh string bag she wore clipped to her

belt. It looked like a snail, a large white snail. Nothing dangerous *there*, certainly. Fedora gestured with one hand to convey his congratulations, and swam on. Suddenly, a vast dark shadow clouding over the surface. . . . What the hell would that be? He peered upwards, perplexed, though not for more than a moment. The hull of the *Polarlys*, of course; they were back at their starting-point. He looked to his left and saw Elsa's brown near-naked body swinging upwards, rising towards the surface with the speed of a demon king disappearing in the last act of a pantomime; then Trout, making rather heavier weather of it, rising in pursuit. Johnny, too, began to plough his way upwards; another strange sensation—having to swim for the surface instead of bobbing straight up like a cork. The lead weights, of course. Might be awkward, that, if one were tired.

Even so, he broke surface fast enough to throw his arms and shoulders clear of the water, and one of his ears gave a disapproving pop. Elsa was already scrambling up the rope-ladder that led to the deck; Trout was treading water at the foot, waiting for him. He spat the breathing-tube out of his mouth, pulled fresh air into his lungs. "Good, wasn't it?" he said. "We ought to have tried it before."

"Well, we have," said Trout.

"I know, but it's different here. You can *see* things. I'm going to take this up."

"It's one way of keeping out the rain."

They climbed up to the deck, carrying their flippers looped over their left forearms. Elsa had spread out on a canvas the contents of her bag, and the Professor was kneeling beside her in a posture suggestive of a broody hen about to lay an egg. He and Elsa poked the various specimens to and fro with their fingertips and conversed in staccato German; Johnny leaned over Elsa's bare brown shoulder to examine the collection more closely. "What was the one you showed me?"

"This. A burrowing snail. Common, but not always easy to find."

"It looked different down there."

"Yes. Prettier. They always do."

The Professor picked up the smooth white shell, traced its convolutions with a fingernail. "Natica," he said, "*Natica alderi*. Yes, is very widespread. Carnivorous, you know. Will attack small bivalves; bores a hole through the shell, inserts proboscis, eats up. A fierce animal, you see." He chuckled obscenely into his beard. "Is interesting as it bores its hole by means of chemical agencies contained in special gland. The dog-whelk—you remember I tell you about the dog-whelk, nucella?—it does the same thing but bores with a lingual ribbon. Process is mechanical." He paused to consider for a moment, as though suspecting that the topic of methods of boring might hold some other, unrelated connotation. "Nucella and natica are two very terrible killers, although they don't look it. In the sea is the same law as on the land. Kill or be killed. You will have thought the life underwater to be calm, peaceful, tranquil. Not so."

Elsa stood up and moved casually a pace or two, removing her swimming-helmet and letting her hair fall loose to her shoulders in a rich, dark, sun-catching cascade. "I suppose," said Johnny, watching her, "there's nothing in these waters dangerous to human beings?"

"Oh no," said the Professor. "Fish are like wild animals. They rarely attack unless they are first attacked, or unless there is blood in the water. Sharks, not even. Though some fish, of course, are curious. Especially the octopus. The octopus is . . . is . . . " He looked at Elsa. ". . . *Wissbegierig*."

"Inquisitive."

"Yes, yes, is an *inquisitive* animal. Are many in these waters, but very small ones. They don't represent a danger." His eyes again grew pale and thoughtful behind their pebbled lenses, as though some other new idea had entered his mind; then he, too, got to his feet, wiping his fingers on the front of his shirt. ". . . Tonight, gentlemen, we have a little party. This is for members of the expedition, strictly speaking. But we shall be pleased if you will also come."

"A party?"

"Yes, yes, a little wine-drinking, that's all, but we shall be pleased to have you."

"Tonight?"

"Yes, tonight," said Elsa. "Please come. It is nice for us to entertain strangers. It makes a change."

"Well, thank you," said Fedora. "We'd like to come."

THREE hundred feet above the coastline, the Sikorsky helicopter shuddered as it ploughed through the after-dusk vectors of warm rising air; Valera, crouched down in the cupola, was beginning to feel a little sick, though naturally he did his best to conceal that fact. It had been a long flight; Malaga to Cadiz, and now back again, with innumerable investigatory detours and circlings. Nothing to report. Now it was dark, or very nearly, and the sea a black pall of sullen movement stretched out to the south. The darkness made little difference from the patroller's viewpoint; the radar picked out with perfect accuracy every spot on the sea larger than a floating seagull. But the radar was the concern of one man only, its operator; Valera could see nothing now, and he felt tired, useless, hungry, cramped and bored, more or less in that order of urgency.

The radio ticked out a message somewhere in front and, after a pause, the observer turned in his seat to hand Valera the scrawled message. Nothing unaccounted for; the same as usual. The coast patrols would be broadcasting the same message on their walkie-talkies. Valera glanced sideways at his companion, uncertain whether or not to wake him up; then saw that the round toad-like eyes with their flat lids were wide open. "Nothing unaccounted for," he said. "That's from Bible Four at Estepona. We won't hear anything else from them before we get to Malaga."

Acuña yawned. "Awwwwww," he said.

"We're drawing a rain cheque, aren't we? Either he's sitting good and tight, or else he's got away already."

"Or else," said Acuña lazily, "he's got a good cover. What did you expect?"

The helicopter droned on. A pale glow of light was visible now some way ahead; the lights of Marbella; and the village lighthouse stabbed its silver cone at them three times swiftly, then died out into blackness. "Marbella," said Valera, as though to himself. Then, "Why don't you let me try that hunch?"

"Because it's probably wrong," said Acuña. "And because even if it's right, we'd risk scaring them. I don't want to scare them. I want to spot them. That's all."

"That's where he lived, towards the end of the war. In that Anteojo place. He was sent there. I don't have to tell you what for."

"No," said Acuña. "You don't have to tell me what for."

"Well, it's a hunch."

"I know," said Acuña. "A hunch. *I* have them, some-times."

A few moment's silence, except for the growl of the engine and the firm swinging beat of the great vanes above them . . . noises to which they had grown so accustomed over the last few hours as to be able to accept them as silence itself. Then the observer leaned back again towards Valera. "Radar's picking up some-thing," he said. "Something we don't know about."

"Where?"

"Straight ahead. Maybe two hundred yards off the coast."

Valera pushed himself sideways, peering out and

downwards. He saw it almost at once, and at the same time as the observer. A small pool of silver on the sea, the reflection of powerful arc lamps on the water's surface. He made a faintly disgusted noise in his throat. "*Nada*," he said. "Another bloody fishing-boat."

"It's by itself," said the observer. Valera stared down through the perspex once more. Yes, that part of it was unusual. "Take its position," he said.

"*Ya lo he hecho.*" The observer passed back the mapping pad, a spider's web of connecting compass references, and tapped it with the point of his pencil. Valera studied it with increasing interest, then leaned sideways to stare downwards yet again; the boat had already disappeared behind them, and more pools of silver light were coming into view farther out at sea. "There's some more of them," said the observer cheerfully.

Valera took no notice. He nudged Acuña's elbow. "Here, look at this. That one must have been fishing pretty nearly dead opposite this Anteojo place . . . if he *was* fishing. Can we take another look at him?"

"Why?"

"I want to see if there are any lights showing on shore."

"There weren't," said Acuña. "I looked."

"None at all?"

"None at all."

"All the same . . . that's where El Anteojo *is*."

Acuña grunted. "Oh yes. I saw it. I saw a flash of white, anyway. Could only have been a house. But no lights. And that's odd, because there's someone living there."

"Maybe they go early to bed."

"Do they hell."

"You mean you know who they are?" said Valera, beginning to grin a tight internal grin that his face did nothing to reveal. Whatever it was you thought of, Acuña would always have thought of it first. The damned old fox.

"Yes, I know who they are. Daughter of an Argentine millionaire and a couple of boy friends."

"*Two* boy friends?" said Valera, and whistled under his breath. "My God. These South Americans."

"She left a couple of weeks back. But her pals are still there. They both once worked for the British Intelligence Services."

Valera's lips stayed puckered up, as though he had been frozen into that position by a blast from a Martian ray-gun. "Oh no," he said. "Oh no. We can't have *that*."

"Not much we can do about it. Their passports are in order." Acuña frowned, joggled his left foot up and down. "All right. I'm buying this one. You go down there tomorrow and get your nose to the ground. Check on that boat with the local patrols. But be damned careful how you play it, that's all. It may interest you to know that someone went to see Heredia this morning—someone we don't know about. At any rate, no one seemed able to place him."

"Heredia?"

Acuña clicked his tongue. "Bruniev."

"Oh, Bruniev. And it's somebody. . . . ?"

"It isn't just the rank and file who drift in to chat with Bruniev," said Acuña impatiently. "As yet I can't be sure, but I've got a sneaking feeling it was Fera-montov. If it was . . . then this is what we've been hoping for. And it'll give you some idea of what you're up against."

Valera looked down at his hands, which lay in his lap. He clenched and unclenched them lightly, conscious of an unpleasant feeling in his stomach as though he had suddenly swallowed a block of ice. "Feramontov," he said. "I see." A nice thing to have slung at one casually, just like that. "All right. I'll be careful."

"Yes," said Acuña. "You'd better."

UNDER the swinging circles of the Klieg lights, the smooth sea bubbled and heaved. Feramontov leaned out over the bulwarks, staring downwards; then reached over to snap off all but the riding lights. His green cat's eyes swiftly accustomed themselves to the sudden darkness; he saw a hand appear on the side of the boat, another come grasping up to join it. Feramontov moved aft, helped Moreno aboard; turned to start the motor. Moreno lay at full length on the boards, the rubber diving-mask pushed up high over his forehead, gasping.

Feramontov said, "Where are they?"

Moreno loosened the string bag at his belt. "Here."

"All of them?"

"Yes, all."

"Good."

Feramontov swung his hip hard against the tiller as the engine picked up, steering the dinghy expertly away from the line of semi-phosphorescent foam marking the rocks on the beachline. A row of distant lights came into view as they rounded the little headland; the other night fishers, farther out to sea. Moreno had almost recovered his breath now; he sat up, kicked the rubber flippers away from his feet. "What was that came over?"

"A helicopter."

"Does that mean trouble?"

"No way of knowing." Feramontov shrugged. "And you?"

"A very little. Hardly worth mentioning."

He slipped from his shoulders the canvas straps, the near-exhausted compressed-air tubes; took off the diving-mask, then the weighted belt with its dangling geologist's hammer and broad-bladed chisel. His fingers caressed the wooden handle for several moments before relinquishing it. Feramontov watched him closely, studying the blur of his raised face profiled against the bubbling white slash of the dinghy's wake. But Moreno said nothing more. He whistled instead, under his breath, almost inaudibly; and began to put on his shirt.

"ONE never dives alone," Elsa was saying. "That is rule number one. So many things can happen. One never knows. It's rather like mountaineering. One takes no unnecessary risks."

Fedora tried a little more of the Fino Oloroso and then leaned back, feeling comfortable. He stared vaguely round the room. By now, the party was well under way; the dining-table, which earlier had been laden with all variety of condiments from cold tortillas to fried shrimps, had been largely denuded, and the staggering display of wine-bottles along the dresser was diminishing even faster. Fedora himself was getting the slightest bit tiddly. He didn't care.

Elsa, who had been standing to his right, now sat down beside him on the sofa, crossing her long brown legs and pulling down her skirt. She was wearing a dress now, a pink dress with a wide red Turkish sash and with a matching red turban of towelling over her still-damp hair; on most other girls it might have been called demure, but on her it certainly didn't seem to be.

"You look nice in that," said Johnny, focusing on her with an effort. "It suits you."

"Thank you. I like it because it is comfortable. Though nowadays I am most comfortable in a bathing suit."

"Well, you look nice in a bathing suit, too."

She looked at him for a moment before replying. Johnny noticed then—and was surprised by—the darkness of the pupils of her eyes; they were Eastern rather than Nordic, he thought, hinting perhaps at a touch of Slavonic blood. "I *do* know how to flirt, Mr. Fedora, if that is what you are wondering. One can be an efficient scientist and still know how to flirt. *Ist nicht unvereinbar.*"

Johnny smiled. "All right," he said. "Let's flirt. But not in German."

"I agree. For that, German is not suitable. I am sorry, though—I don't speak English very well."

"Too many ones."

"What?"

"You use the construction with 'One' too much. If you say, 'One knows how to flirt,' it sounds so impersonal that nobody'll believe it."

"I see. Then what should one. . . . ?"

"What should you say?"

"Yes, what should I say?"

"It's not so much what you say. It's how you say it."

"Yes, I appreciate that. Well, then. I am very very glad you could come tonight to our party. Because it is nice for me to get away from my work from time to time, like this, and to talk to a . . . a . . . "

"Handsome and talented young man."

". . . To a handsome and talented young man such as yourself. Yes. How am I doing?"

"Not bad. Perhaps a bit more feeling."

"Feeling? All right. Who feels? Me or you?"

"I will," said Johnny with alacrity. "Shoulder, perhaps, to start with? Or do you prefer the knee?"

"Initially, I think, the hand."

"Oh Lord." Fedora readjusted his posture. "That's rather a disappointment."

"The second of the day."

"The second?"

"Yes. Mr. Trout was disappointed this morning, I couldn't help thinking, when I didn't wear my bikini."

"You're not allowed to, are you? In Spain?"

"No, that's why I didn't. I am not a girl who *likes* to disappoint."

"I shouldn't worry," said Fedora. "Anyone who's disappointed at you in a bathing suit ought to see either an optician or a neurologist. My God, here comes the Professor."

"Ah, the Professor," repeated Elsa dreamily. "He is a duck."

Fedora found this remark so totally unexpected that he stared at her open-mouthed. He had time to say nothing more before the Professor was alongside; he was holding in his hand—or not so much holding as flourishing—an empty wineglass, and his expression was convivial in the extreme. "Ah, *gna' Fraulein*," said he, in an outburst of old-world gallantry. "Aha, my dear boy! So charming the party, the atmosphere, our hospitality! Yah, yah! Enchanted, enchanted."

Fedora stood up. "Let me fill your glass for you, Professor."

"Ah, this vine, this vine! *Merkwerdig! Ich konnte mich jetzt betrinken wie zwei Matrosen*," said the Professor, relinquishing the glass. "*Und es wurde mir gut tun*. Ha ha! Ha ha!"

"Perhaps you'd better. . . . I mean, won't you sit down, Professor?"

"*Danke, danke*," said the Professor, collapsing on to

the sofa and slapping Elsa heartily on the back. "My little helper! You know my little helper?"

"We have indeed met," said Fedora. "Er. . . . Charming."

"Charming, *tjaaa*, a charming girl, a good girl. And very sound, what's more, biologically speaking."

"You're telling me," said Fedora. "If you'll excuse me a moment, I'll get you another drink."

"A small one, a small one! Already the mouth can with the wineglass difficultly in contact come!" The Professor gestured wildly, preparing to embark on yet another complicated stretch of syntax; Johnny, forestalling him, stepped smartly away. The movement brought a sudden prickle of perspiration to his forehead. Some fresh air, he decided, would be just the thing.

He handed the glass to one of the white-coated stewards who stood by the dresser. "For the Professor," he said. "A little wine and the rest, *gaseosa*. Otherwise it'll be a lucky break for the jellyfish." Then he walked fairly quickly towards the door, bumping lightly into Meuvret; who was regaling Trout with a long description of some piscatorial or amatory exploit, his hands sketching in the air a rapid outline of what might have been either a sting-ray or an anatomically spectacular Frenchwoman. "Going out?" said Trout, looking up. "Just for a moment," said Johnny.

He went down the passage towards the deck. When he was halfway along, a door to his right opened and a big man came out; a big man in a white shirt and grey flannel trousers. His head was lowered towards the deck, and he saw Fedora only in time to avoid walking straight into him. Then he stopped short; and the two men, not a foot apart, stared at each other. Then, after a moment, the big man smiled.

"Been having fun?"

"Yes, thanks," said Fedora.

The big man went on smiling. "That's right," he said. "So have I."

He turned away, stepped back into the room he had just left and closed the door. Fedora realised suddenly that his cheek muscles had gone tight . . . that he, too, was smiling, though not in a way that he could immediately recognise. He leaned abruptly forward to read the card in the slot by the door: *Jaime Baroda*, it said.

Fedora stepped back and wiped his forehead. He was probably rather drunker than he'd realised. Well . . . a breath of fresh air, a last glass of wine, and then it would be time to go home. It hadn't been a bad party, at that. He walked on to the end of the corridor, put his weight against the door and stepped out on to the deck.

THE car drew up outside the house a little before midnight. Trout sat back in the driving-seat to knuckle his eyes, then opened the door and got out. "My God," he said, staring belligerently at the wavering outlines of the front door and breathing cognac fumes into the atmosphere. "My God, I'm pickled."

"You might have told me that before you started driving," said Fedora.

"Switching to cognac, that's what did it. Quite a party, eh? Quite a party."

Johnny didn't feel that he had anything useful to add to the conversation at this stage in the proceedings. He got the doorkey out of his pocket, manoeuvred it into the lock. They went in. Johnny collapsed on the sofa.

"That goddam cognac," said Trout, tramping round the room like an energetic elephant. "That's what did me in. The cognac. Let's put the radio on, hey, dance a bit, sober up. Hey?"

Johnny groaned. "Dance who with? Me?"

"Oh well, there's that. Thought you were doing all right, too."

"What?" said Fedora, failing to follow.

"With what's-her-name. Nice little girl, that. Going on to cognac, that was my mistake, odsbodikins," said Trout, flapping his arms to and fro like a Polar explorer warming himself up. "Jewish blood there somewhere, I wouldn't mind betting."

"What blood? Who?"

"That girl. Elsa. The German one. Anyway, there wasn't any other, you *must* know who I mean." Trout's eyes focused horribly on a point in the air about one yard in front of his nose. "I say, I feel awful."

"You look awful. Let's have a shower."

"Good idea. No, let's all go down to the swimming-pool and take a quick dick, I said a quip *dip*. Jus' to stone us up a little."

"No, I want a shower."

"No, let's have a swim."

"Don't want to."

"Well, *I*'m going."

"Well, *go* then."

"All right," said Trout, offended.

Fedora immediately rose and went out through the bathroom door. There was a few moments' silence. Then a sudden agonising blast of orchestral music indicated that Fedora had pressed the wrong switch again; Trout, who was definitely not in the mood for that sort of thing, clutched at his head with a hunted expression and bounded out of the room. Fedora, searching feverishly over the control panel, at last managed to cut the music off in mid-crescendo and to get the shower turned on: silence descended again, except for the fast fluid gushing noise of the water. Johnny stripped off his clothes, raised his head, screwed up his eyes and stepped in. *Ahhhhhh*. That was better. Except that he couldn't breathe. He fumbled for the key; a faint whining noise showed that he had succeeded only in devaporising the shaving-mirror. A further frantic scrabble increased, if anything, the velocity of the cascading water and turned it on the instant to an icy coldness; whimpering faintly, Fedora leapt away and towards his bathrobe. His head ached rather worse than before, but at least the cobwebs had disappeared. He towelled himself down and then, returning, switched off in succession both the water and the devaporiser. Pleased at this success, he went through to his bedroom and fell face downwards on the bed. Now, he thought, it would be nice to go to sleep.

He was, in fact, on the point of dropping off when the door opened with a startled jerk and Trout shot into the room, stopping so abruptly that his hair flipped down over his eyes. He was very wet and was wearing his bathing shorts. Also he was looking at Johnny, and his eyes weren't out of focus at all. ". . . Johnny."

Fedora's feet were already swinging, very fast, off the bed. "What's the matter?"

"In our pool. There's a girl there. She's dead."

"What, drowned?"

"No, no. It's not an accident."

"Phone the police, then."

"You think so?"

"Yes, of course."

Trout went. Johnny pulled on his shirt, his trousers and a pair of sandals; then flipped open the brown pigskin travelling-case at the foot of the bed and took the Mauser pistol from its clip. He didn't know exactly how bad things were, but Trout was obviously stone-cold sober and that had to mean something. He went through to the sitting-room, where Trout was talking very fast, in Spanish, to the telephone. ". . . *SI, hombre, si. Asesinada, ya lo he dicho dos veces. Bueno, y a mi que me*

*importa la hora que es? . . . Pues claro que vendrá en seguida,
le estamos esperando.*"

He jammed down the receiver, pushed his wet hair
back from his forehead. "Murdered?" said Johnny.
"You're sure?"

"Of course I'm sure." Trout hesitated. "It's one of
those."

"What d'you mean, one of *those?*"

"Well, the body's naked and it's all cut about and
the blood's just everywhere. . . . It turned me up, it
really did."

"It turned you up? But *you*'ve seen a few, haven't
you?"

"Yes, but nothing like this. Look," said Trout,
holding out his right foot with repugnance. There were
red sticky smears over the instep and running up his
shin; Fedora stared at them as though mesmerised.
"You mean it's still wet?" he said. "The wound's still
open?"

"It's in the pool. The pool's full of it."

Johnny opened the hall cupboard and took out a
torch, then opened the front door. The night outside
was filled with the scent of mimosa. "I suppose it was
too dark for you to see if it was anyone we know?"

"I can't be sure. She hasn't any head."

"No *head?*"

"Well, I couldn't find it. But I didn't hang around
to hunt. If it happened in the pool, maybe a head by
itself would sink. I don't know."

Fedora nodded. "Yes," he said. "It would."

They followed the beam of the torch down the crazy-
paving path to the pool. It gleamed then on polished
tiles, on rubber matting, on the steel and concrete of

the diving-ramp; and on something small and white and
wet and glistening that lay at the edge of the pool, half-
in and half-out the water. "Is that how you found her?"

"No. She was floating. I pulled her in a bit . . . not
all the way because I had to stop and be sick. Got rid
of all that blasted cognac, anyway."

They stopped. The torch beam focused steadily on
the thing at their feet, and Johnny felt his own stomach
lurch uneasily. "God," he said. "I'm not surprised."

"It's horrible, isn't it? You ought to turn her over
and see . . . underneath. You'd say an *animal* did it."

"Knifed?"

"Knifed? Gouged, more like it. Cut right open . . .
you know. Oh, it's one for the textbooks all right, it
really is."

"Sex maniac," said Fedora between his teeth. "How
frightfully jolly for us. I suppose we'd better look for
the head, Tiddler."

"Can't we leave that to the police? It's got nothing
to do with us, has it?"

"It's our damned pool," said Fedora.

"Yes, but—"

"And besides, I think I know who it is."

"You do?"

Fedora knelt down, lifted the girl's cold right hand
and touched the ring on her third finger. The tiny
white chip of stone winked derisorily against the dull
band of copper. "It's Carmen," he said. "The maid."

"Carmen? But aren't there *two* of them?"

"The other one's not here tonight. She went to see
her family in Estepona. Of course, a lot of girls wear
rings like this, but it looks like Carmen to me. The
build's about right."

"Carmen, but hell, I *liked* Carmen."

"So did I," said Johnny. "Even if I didn't, I still wouldn't have cared for anything like *this* to happen to her. Come on. Help me lift her out."

"Oh Lord. No, leave her as she is."

"You said you liked her." Fedora looked up. "You really feel like leaving everything to the police?"

There was a moment's silence. Then Trout stooped down, felt for the girl's naked shoulders with his big blunt fingers. The body didn't weigh very much. They heaved once together, and she was out, lying on her back on the cool colourless tiles of the parquet flooring. Fedora's breath began to rasp at the back of his throat. "Yes," he said thickly. "Yes, I see what you meant."

Trout straightened up again and walked away, wiping his hands automatically against his bathing shorts. Fedora took the torch in his left hand, leaned down over the corpse. His eyes were glazed over now with a kind of impassive intentness, were almost cruel in their total concentration on the object before them. The torch beam moved steadily over the girl's body, from pathetically twisted feet to truncated neck. In the end, Fedora reached down to pull apart the limp, narrow thighs, began to explore with his fingers the gaping pink mouths with grey edges that radiated from the shadows of her underbelly. Trout came back and stood at his side, but didn't try to look at what he was doing.

"You were right," said Fedora suddenly. "It wasn't a knife."

"No?"

"No. No cutting edge. These aren't slashes. The belly's been torn open from inside, as far as I can see.

Four times, in four different directions. That must take a bit of strength. She was dead first, that's the only consolation."

"You think so?"

"These wounds haven't bled. Hardly at all. So it must have been when he cut her head off . . . though that's just the same. Tearing, more than cutting. Sort of ripped."

"Yes. That word has unfortunate conno-connotations." Trout was beginning to feel the cold; his teeth were chattering lightly.

"There has to be a lot of blood about somewhere, Tiddler."

"There is. In the pool. I told you. I was swimming along in there, couldn't make out what the hell it was."

"Yes. Well, look at this."

"I'd rather not."

"*This* is a clean cut. You can see where the ripping commences. I can tell you what he did it with."

"All right, what?"

"Something like a chisel."

"A *chisel?*"

Fedora measured the macerated flesh with his bent thumb. "Yes. A one-inch chisel, I'd say. Allowing for a degree of muscular contraction. That's about the only thing that'd make a mess like this."

Trout nodded. "Funny thing for someone to be carrying round, though, wouldn't you say?"

"Yes. True." Fedora looked up sharply. "We'd better go back to the house. And you'd better get changed. Unless you want a go of pneumonia."

"It's not that cold. Besides, what about the head?"

"Never mind the head," said Johnny. "I've changed my mind."

THE Provincial Judge was a pleasant-looking middle-aged fellow, with greying hair and the commencement of a jowl; he had met Fedora several times before and his attitude now was cautiously amicable. He sat in one of the grey-and-red Knoll armchairs in the sitting-room and talked about this and that while the police doctor was examining the corpse and while the police sergeant was hunting for clues—more particularly for the head. His manner suggested that the finding of dismembered cadavers in the swimming-pool was just another of the minor inconveniences attached to life in the deep south, along with the mosquitoes, the *levante* and the water shortage. But he was really perplexed and, at times, his guard slipped and he showed it.

When both the doctor and the sergeant had returned to make their reports, (the head had been found in the short grass a few yards from the pool, where it had presumably been either dropped or thrown), he questioned Johnny and Trout briefly as to the circumstances of their discovery and as to their previous movements throughout the evening. He didn't seem to expect that their answers would help in any way to elucidate his problem, and though he kept his notebook open on his lap, he didn't use it at all.

"*Bueno*," he said, at the end. "That's all very clear. Not much doubt as to your alibi, anyway." And he closed the notebook and put it away in his pocket.

"Not, of course, that I'm suggesting you could have had anything to do with it. But offhand, to be frank, we'd be inclined to suspect foreigners, just because of the method. This kind of... of business is very rare in these parts, it really is. Whereas the Americans seem to go in for it wholesale, if the magazines one reads are anything to go by. And the Germans, of course. A very thorough-going race, the Germans. Well, we'll have to make inquiries, won't we? ... and see what results we get. Her parents live in Fuengirola, I believe. We'll notify them. Yes, I'll get in touch with you later. No need to worry. A very sad business, very regrettable, but no need for you to worry. None at all."

... The police doctor was waiting outside in the car. The judge got in beside him, mopping his forehead with a handkerchief. "That's that," he said. "*Qué canallada.*"

"Messy," said the doctor. "Very messy. *Vamonos.*"

The driver rolled the car forward down the drive, and they set off for the village. It was almost two o'clock. The doctor yawned.

"We'll manage a formal identification in the morning," said the judge. "Meantime I'll take your word as to who it is. Or rather, was. D'you know anything about her? She been seen out with anyone lately?"

"She's got a *novio.* Juanito Garcia."

"Who's he?"

"Fisherman. You know the Garcias. Three brothers, they own that boat down by the Faro."

"Ah."

"I never heard anything against her. Or against him, either."

The judge took out his handkerchief again, this time to blow his nose. "Working for foreigners, though."

"Lots of 'em do."

"I know. But I've noticed that it often leads to a certain weakening of the moral fibre. This Garcia, he probably wouldn't have liked it over-much."

"You think she. . . . ?"

"It seems likely enough." The judge shrugged. "We'll have to be careful how we go, all the same. That house belongs to the señorita Tocino, and she has all manner of connections in the government. And money —*caramba*—that's obvious. You notice anything else about the Englishmen?"

"Well, they seemed very calm."

"*Exactly*. You'd think they turned up mutilated bodies every damned day of the blasted week. I know Englishmen are phlegmatic and all that, but I've never seen anything like *those* two. Inhuman, I call it."

"I don't know," said the doctor slowly. "The dark-haired one—he was angry. *Very* angry. Maybe he was the one who slept with her. Either way, I wouldn't much care to be in Juanito Garcia's shoes right now— unless I had a very good alibi."

"I didn't notice that he was angry," said the judge, after a thoughtful pause.

"He was angry inside."

They had reached the village now, and the car swung sharp left to head for the Plaza Central; the narrow whitewashed street it entered was silent, deserted. The judge lit a cigarette and the lighter flame etched out his face's reflection sharply in the window. "Well, I'll see Garcia in the morning," he said. "Maybe we'll have no trouble. But unless it clears itself up right away, it'll have to go to Malaga. One can't be too careful where foreigners are concerned."

"Very true," said the doctor.

THERE was no early-morning coffee the next day, because there was no Carmen to make it and serve it. Trout and Johnny, all the same, were both up early. Trout went to the kitchen to experiment with grinders and percolators, while Fedora put on his shirt, trousers and sandals and went round to the servants' wing. Trout found him there ten minutes later, sitting morosely on Carmen's truckle bed and investigating the contents of a brown cardboard suitcase lying open on the floor at his feet. The servants' quarters at El Anteojo were much more comfortable than most, but as bare as Spanish tradition demanded. A coloured picture of the Giralda at Sevilla and another of the Virgin Mary, both cut out of a cheap magazine and pasted on plywood, hung on the wall above the bed and seemed to be about the only adornments that Carmen's room had to offer. There were a couple of photographs, however, under the glass top of the bedside table; one of a fat, elderly lady dressed entirely in black—presumably her mother—and another of a black-haired youth in Spanish military uniform, leaning on a rock and squinting cheerfully into the sun. Trout put the coffee-pot down on the dresser and mooched idly around for a few moments without speaking; then sat down on the bed beside Fedora. "Had any bright ideas, Johnny?"

"I was just wondering what she wore last night. That's all."

"What she *wore?*"

"Well, she wouldn't have gone out naked, would she?—the way you found her? Still, that's what she was wearing yesterday." Johnny pointed to the chair at the end of the bed, where a calico print dress and a cotton slip lay neatly folded. "Both her uniforms are in the wardrobe, and her nightdress is right here under the pillow. So I think she must have been wearing a swimsuit."

"Likely enough," said Trout, "if it happened at the pool."

"Yes. Let's say she went out for a swim, then, last thing at night. Down at the pool. Now either she'd arranged to meet somebody there, or else somebody just happened to be around. The first idea isn't very likely." Johnny glanced shortly towards the photographs on the table, looked away again. "If she fixed up anything like that, I doubt if it was with her *novio*. Girls don't *do* that sort of thing around these parts, not with the men they're going to marry. She might have arranged to meet someone else, but I doubt that, too. If she had, she'd almost certainly have worn something else apart from just a swimsuit. Which leaves us with the question of what a complete stranger would have been doing round here at that time of the night."

"Rubbernecking," suggested Trout.

"You think so?"

"Why not? There *are* people like that, you know. Who hang round private swimming-pools in the hope of catching some woman or other in the rude. My God," said Trout forcefully, "there has to be something pretty seriously *wrong* with whoever it was who did it. You've got to remember *that*."

"It was pretty dark last night, though, wasn't it? He

couldn't have hoped to see very much that way."

"I don't know. With a good pair of night-glasses. . . ."

"And a chisel?"

"What? Well, but you can't be *sure* it was a chisel."

Fedora sighed. "I got up before you did, this morning," he said. "Quite a long time before." He pushed himself up to his feet. "Come on. I'll show you something."

"What?"

"You'll see."

Trout followed him out into the open, privately thinking that it was still a little early in the morning for this kind of brainwork. They rounded the pergola and set off down the path towards the pool, Fedora whistling under his breath. "She'd have come this way," he said, "to get to the pool. Not that it matters a lot."

They reached the tiled surrounds of the pool and came to a halt by the diving-ramp. The pool was empty. "Did you do that?" asked Trout, staring.

Johnny nodded. "That's what I meant when I said that I'd got up early. It took me all of fifteen minutes to find out how the hydraulics worked. It dried out in no time, though, once I'd got it going."

"Good idea," said Trout, sniffing the air dubiously. "The thing could do with a real scrubbing-out, if you ask me. They say there's only ten pints of blood in the human body. . . . All I can say is, if you'd been swimming in there with me last night you'd find it pretty hard to believe, too."

"That wasn't why I did it, though."

"No? Then why?"

"Curiosity."

"Curiosity?"

"Look," said Fedora. He pointed.

The sun was as yet hardly risen and the lower parts of the pool were in deep shadow; Trout had to lean forward and stare hard to see what Johnny was indicating, and even after he had seen it he was by no means sure just what it was. "What the hell is it?"

"It's a hole."

"I can see it's a hole, but . . . Is that where the water runs out?"

"No, that's the drainage pipe. Over there."

"Well then, what's *that* hole doing there?"

"That's what *I*'d like to know," said Johnny. "Let's go down there and see if you have any brainwaves."

They clambered down the steps and walked across the cool smooth floor of the pool. The hole was at the deepest part of the pool, near where they had been standing and almost directly under the diving-ramp. Two of the tiles in the wall, not in the lowest row but in the next lowest, had disappeared, leaving behind a deep cemented recess. Trout got down on hands and knees to peer into it. "Anything inside?"

"Nothing. I've looked."

"Well, but then. . . . " Trout suddenly reached out to finger the chipped cement of the tiles immediately below the recess. "*Now* I see what you meant."

"Yes. That's where it slipped." Johnny pointed to a sharp-edged scratch on the surface of one of the tiles. "And cut through the glaze. A one-inch chisel, near as makes no difference. I measured it."

"It looks like some kind of a hiding-place."

"That's what I thought, too."

"And a good one, at that. You've got to let all the water out to get at it, haven't you?"

"Or work under water."

"Would that be possible?"

"For a good diver, yes. That's how I think it happened. He was down here working when Carmen went in. She wouldn't have seen him or noticed anything that way, not until she was actually in the pool. And then it was too late. Poor kid."

"He killed her . . . just because she found him there?"

"I think so," said Johnny.

"But then why the . . . the refinements?"

"Maybe he wanted to make it look like another kind of crime altogether. To put people off the scent, so to speak. I've got the idea that the way he killed her in the first place was kind of recognisable . . . and so he had to disguise his handiwork a bit. Make it look messy, when it was really as neat as you like. Of course," said Johnny, "he didn't have to be so thorough. There's something wrong with him all right—that's true enough."

Trout was no fool; he was aware of the implications of what Fedora was saying long before Fedora had finished speaking. "When you said *recognisable*," he said slowly, ". . . ?"

"Somebody's been doing some very recognisable killing around Malaga lately," said Johnny.

"Moreno."

"Yes."

"But what would Moreno be mucking about in our swimming-pool for?"

"I'd like to know that, too," said Johnny. He stood up, and they began to mount once more the steps of the pool. "Up to a point I can put two and two together, but it doesn't make four yet or anything like it. Still, something was hidden there. That seems obvious. And you know who this place belonged to before Adriana's father got hold of it?"

"No, who?"

"A Spaniard called Priego. Another millionaire. He made most of his money in the war, servicing and supplying U-boats on the Mediterranean run. Well, and Moreno worked for him at one time. Handing on the information to Soviet Intelligence."

"Yes, I knew that last bit. I saw his file once. But was he working *here?*"

"That's what I don't know. But it seems likely enough. They call this place El Anteojo—the Spyglass— because it covers the whole damned Straits of Gibraltar as far as Ceuta. You couldn't want a better observation post to pick up the Malta convoys." Fedora pushed open the door of Carmen's room again, turned to look back at Trout. "The thing I like least is the business of that cache's having been fifteen feet underwater."

"Why?"

"Because it makes me think of aqualungs."

He sat down heavily on the bed, ignoring the plaintive squeak of the bedsprings. Trout poured out the coffee, and for a few moments they sipped at their cups contemplatively without saying anything. Eventually,

"I can see what you're *getting* at," said Trout glumly. "But the aqualungs on the *Polarlys* aren't the only ones in Spain, you know. It's a popular sport, round here."

"On the other hand, that party of theirs certainly got us both out of the way very conveniently."

"The only thing wrong with that is that they've all got alibis. We were all there *together*, dammit."

"There was somebody who wasn't. A man called

Jaime Baroda. I met him on the way out. A very big man with dark hair."

Trout rose to stare out of the window. The sun was tangled now in the tops of the palm trees, spattering his face with a pattern of blue shade. "Moreno?"

"He could have been. I had a sort of feeling about him, even then. . . . You know what I mean?"

"I ought to, by now."

"Another thing. *They*'ve got some chisels. We saw them."

"Jesus," said Trout. His head jerked round abruptly into the full glare of the sun. "So we did."

"They've got a whole lot of equipment. Equipment that you could use for hunting something rather bigger than jellyfish."

"Such as. . . . ?"

"U-boats, for instance," said Fedora.

". . . Skin in the fingernails," said Valera. "It's a useful pointer, of course. But I'm surprised, all the same."

"It's very frequent in these cases," said the Provincial Judge.

"The man I'm thinking of doesn't usually give them that much time. Of course, it was dark, and presumably he killed her in the water. Had to get hold of her first. But even so."

"It's a let-out for young Garcia, anyway," said the Judge. "I had him in here first thing this morning. But there wasn't a scratch on him that was less than a fortnight old. Well, and now you've come along with this very disturbing new idea—which I certainly don't say is likely to be wrong, but which gives us a whole lot of things to think about. Obviously, if you're right, it isn't a sex killing at all. Are we supposed to be able to guess at the true motive?"

He sounded rather bitter, thought Valera. The old complaint, of course. The old, familiar jibes at excessive centralisation, at the reluctance of the Secret Police to hand out information, to let the left hand know what the right hand was doing. "I suppose you've had Madrid on the telephone," he said; wearily, because he was rather tired.

"Naturally. Oh, we're here to co-operate, you don't have to worry about that. This is just the sort of case

I'm happy to hand over. But it's not much fun for us having a fellow like this Moreno on the rampage round these parts—you can see that. I mean, you tell us how to catch him—you give the *orders*—and the police'll bring him in. All they need to know is what to look for—if you follow me."

"It's not as easy as that," said Valera. "I wish it were."

He walked over to the window. The canary in its green-painted cage opened one eye and chirruped at him in sudden panic; he drew aside the muslin curtains, looked out into the sundrenched village square. "What about that boat?" he asked.

"We haven't located it yet. It wasn't any of the local fishermen, though—that's been established."

Valera came back, sat down at the old-style mahogany desk with its huge carved legs and leather blotter. He wouldn't have liked the Judge's job; not at all. He'd have liked it as little as Acuña's. The one too big and the other too small. His own job should have been just right for him, but there were times when he didn't like that, either. "You've seen the people who live there?"

"At El Anteojo? Yes."

"What's your impression?"

"Well, the place belongs to a Señorita Adriana Tocino. She's from the Argentine. But she's not there now. There are only two young Englishmen. The señorita, they tell me, is extremely rich. Her father—"

"I know what the police dossiers say," said Valera, inexorably patient. "I've just finished looking through them. What I wanted from you was your personal impression of these people." He didn't hope for much from it, though. To the judge of a small provincial

village, they'd be simply foreigners, Martians, beings
from another world. He'd have to go and see them for
himself. "How did they react, for instance, to the
murder?"

"Very strangely."

"Strangely?"

"Very calm, very cool, very. . . . Not exactly as
though it were a matter of no importance, no, not *that*,
but as though it were nothing really . . . out of the
ordinary. One of the men seemed a little angry, I
thought."

"Which one?"

"The darkhaired one. His name escapes me at the
moment."

"Fedora." Valera pulled reflectively at a hangnail
on his right thumb. "He's half Spanish, as a matter of
fact. His father fought with the Reds in the Civil War,
until we had him shot in '37. We know quite a lot about
Sr. Fedora."

"But in that case. . . . "

"Oh, he hasn't any other Communist affiliations.
Quite the contrary, in fact. In what way, precisely, was
he angry?"

The Judge thought for a few moments. "It seems an
odd thing to say, I know, but. . . . Well, he seemed to be
taking it as a—a personal affront. I can't be more
explicit."

"That's very interesting," said Valera.

"Yes?"

"Of course it is. Can *you* think of any reason why he
should take a vulgar sex crime as a personal affront?"

"Not unless his relationship with the girl concerned
was also somewhat . . . personal."

"Yes. I suppose that's possible. But there's been quite a lot about Moreno in the newspapers lately. And if by any chance Fedora has already connected him with this crime, somehow. . . . Well, from what we know of him, I'd say it was quite likely that he'd take *that* personally, too."

The Judge shrugged. "You have information that I haven't," he said, "about Sr. Fedora. It may well be so."

"Either way," said Valera, reaching for his hat, "it's going to be interesting finding out."

FEDORA's fingers moved cautiously over the keyboard of the piano. E flat, E and C as a blues triad; the C minor chord; then down to G on the soft pedal. He played the sequence over and over again, repeating it with infinite concentration and care, a bar and a half of meaningless music aching for the breakaway that never came. The sun came slanting in through the open windows, entering the room at an angle as though to spotlight the lean brown enraptured hands, the black and white keys, the high polish on the piano's surface and its reflection of a tousle-haired, unsmiling face staring down at the flawless perfection of the ivory veneer. "Play something, Johnny," said Trout, "there's a good chap." But the piano kept up its mindless, interminable singing of that single interminable phrase; unvarying, intent. Trout moved his feet uneasily on the carpet. Eventually Fedora took his right hand from the keyboard, found a cigarette, put it in his mouth and lit it; the piano seemed to Trout still to be humming that same series of notes, so accustomed had his ears grown to it.

"Pavanne for a dead parlourmaid," said Johnny.

He suddenly hit a full chord in C major, played the old sequence at high speed and went on, full tilt, into the blues. Trout listened, aware of that insidious theme still hanging on the fringes of the melody, seeming to parody it horribly, almost gruesomely. "*Two nineteen done took my baby 'way,"* sang Fedora, in his curiously throaty black-coffee-ruined tenor. *"Two nineteen took my bab' away, Ol' two seventeen'll bring her back some day."* His right hand dissolved into a ripple of fantastic arpeggios, phantasmagoric, chillingly melancholy. The sunlight seemed suddenly to fade around his fingers; he built in swift, haunted arabesques a dark street in a rainy winter, the beat of the water on the low tin roofs, the fan of red light above the door where, in the shadows, a woman smoked a long sweet-smelling cigarette; then let the scene escape with a slow, elaborate figure in the bass like a sudden swirl of fog. Trout sighed. "All the same," he said, "it isn't funny, really."

"If y'ain't got a dollar," sang Fedora, *"gimme a lousy dime. Said if y'ain't got a dollar, well, gimme jus' a lousy ol' dime.* Now, why does that remind me of General Franco? All right, don't tell me. I remember." His hands jittered crazily over the keys, resolving his subject in a series of impromptu and tenuously connected sketches of staggering technical difficulty. "There you are. Now I bow, looking modest. You know, looking sort of humble, as though I don't know what the hell of a great player I am really. And looking tired at the same time, mind you. Worn out by it all. That's very important. Well, what do you fancy for an encore?"

"You couldn't look half as goddam tired as I feel right now," said Trout pointedly. "I'm getting fed up with sitting round watching you think your great thoughts to yourself. Why don't you fly right and tell me what's supposed to be on the ball?"

"*I* don't know what's on the ball," said Johnny. "That's the trouble." He shook his hands up and down a few times, loosely, from the wrists, then got up from the piano-stool. "What do *you* think we ought to do?"

"We could always tell the police."

"Tell them what?"

"Well. . . . Your suspicions."

"Yes, but the police don't much care for suspicions. They don't much care for any kind of volunteered information, as a rule. Better to wait till we're asked."

"You think we will be?"

"Of course," said Johnny. "Of course." He slumped himself bonelessly down into an armchair, let his head flop back on to the cushions. "They'll be around. Don't worry."

"I thought you didn't like the Spanish police."

"I don't," said Johnny.

"Yet you don't mind working in with them?"

"Nobody's talking about working in with anybody. I want to hear what they've got to say, that's all. Even if it's only, 'Get out of our way.' It looks to me as though we're butting in on a halma game that's being played between two other people. And we can't expect either of the players to like it."

"Well, but who *are* the players? The police *versus* Moreno?"

"It can't be just Moreno."

"Not if you're right about the *Polarlys*." Trout turned his head to watch Fedora curiously. "You think this is something *big*, don't you, Johnny?"

"In what way, big?"

"Big people?"

"Oh yes. Big people."

"Russia?"

"If I had to make a bet, yes, I'd say Russia."

"My God," said Trout. "I don't know that I'm

especially anxious to tangle it up with the Russians, at my time of life. They play kind of a rough game, you know, particularly their overseas crowd."

"They play it the same way as we used to. For keeps." Fedora smiled, a smile that appeared to be of genuine amusement. "If it comes to that, I don't much want to tangle with the Spaniards either. They can be a nasty lot to get on the wrong side of. One way or another, I'm beginning to wish I was back in Chicago in the early forties. . . . I was young enough then to play on both sides at once and even like it. But I can't do that any more. They know me, now."

"Yes," Trout agreed. "The penalties of fame. But still, experience counts for something."

"For something, yes. We're both used to trouble. There's always that."

"But not Russian trouble."

"It can't be all that different. A bullet in the belly hurts a Russian as much as anyone else."

"There aren't any Russians on the *Polarlys*, though."

"We don't *know* there aren't."

"I suppose not. But we *do* know there are some Germans. Could be that some of our old ex-Nazi pals are dreaming something up. Spain's stiff with them, anyway."

Johnny shook his head. "It doesn't smell to me like comic opera."

"Hell, it wasn't comic opera that year in Austria. Don't you remember Mayer? *He* was big time."

"That was a long time ago. Besides, what could that crowd have cooking in Spain that *we* wouldn't know about? No, this is operational stuff, Tiddler. That lot aboard the yacht, they've got plenty of backing. That's obvious."

"They could even have too much for us to handle."

"Yes," admitted Johnny. "They could."

"And in any case, I don't suppose they're going to hang around. If they got what they wanted last night from our pool, they'll be off like a shot, won't they? . . . while we're just sitting round here doing damn-all."

"We're not doing damn-all. We're waiting. It's not the same thing."

"Waiting for *what?*"

"For this fellow, probably."

Trout, too, had heard the faint thrum of the car engine turning into the driveway. He got up and moved across to the window, where the sunlight formed a halo in his fair hair and cast his shadow against the piano. He saw the car grind to a halt outside the front door; a portly man in a grey suit swung himself out of the back seat and marched up the steps. "You were right," said Trout, turning back. "Full marks for once. It's some kind of a cop."

"Plain clothes?"

"Yes."

"Um," said Fedora. He began to whistle, between his teeth, the same theme that he had been playing on the piano, and with the same heartbreaking accuracy. The electric door-bell buzzed quietly in the hall; he went out to open the door. Outside was a brown, corpulent man with thinning hair and faded grey eyes; a high, beaky nose over a clipped moustache; carefully polished black shoes and well-creased trousers. He looked at Fedora, and Fedora looked at him; and comprehension between the two of them was somehow at once complete.

"Sr. Fedora? I am a police officer. My name is Valera."

"Yes," said Johnny. "Come in."

MORENO was breakfasting on liver and bacon, while Elsa sat at the far side of the dining-table and watched him. He took no notice, if indeed he was aware of her scrutiny; he seemed entirely absorbed in the act of eating, an act which appeared to demand not only all his attention but the employment of almost all his facial muscles; with the rhythmic movement of his lips and jaws, sinews writhed high up in his temples, jerked to and fro with the regularity of a nervous tic. The sharp morning light brought his cheekbones into high relief, sculped into a third dimension the outline of wide forehead, broad nose. Eventually he laid down his knife and fork; looked up, not at Elsa but towards the ceiling. "When are we leaving?" he asked.

"The clearance certificate ought to be ready by eleven."

"And then we sail?"

"That's for Feramontov to say. Are you nervous?"

"Do I look nervous?"

"Not at all. That's why I ask. I am interested."

"I'm not nervous. But I don't believe in wasting time."

"I see. You're always eager for the next death. . . . Is that it?"

Moreno wiped his mouth on his napkin. "Somehow it's not a thing one talks about."

"Why not?"

"'One never knows whose the next death will be."

"And why should that matter?"

"A superstition. Call it that, if you like." He poured himself out a glass of milk from the porcelain jug, began to sip at it slowly. "You're not the superstitious kind, though," said Elsa. "You're a schizo. Aren't you?"

"So I've been told."

"You killed someone last night."

Moreno put down the glass. There was a white smear of milk on his upper lip; his tongue flicked out abruptly and licked it away. "Feramontov," he said. "He talks perhaps a little too much."

"Feramontov didn't tell me."

"Then how did you know?"

"I knew. And it was different to the others, wasn't it? A woman?"

Moreno nodded. "There was a girl. Swimming in the pool. And it was necessary to kill her. Afterwards, I cut off her head."

"Why?"

"I've told you . . . one doesn't talk about these things."

"Was she an *attractive* girl, Moreno?"

"I didn't notice."

"Yes, you must have. You must have had to touch her when you killed her, you must have had to hold her. . . . What does it feel like, Moreno, when you touch them and they. . . . What do they do? They scream, don't they? You *wait* for them to scream, don't you? Isn't that what you do?"

"You don't understand," said Moreno, his tongue coming out again and again in search of a smear of grease that was no longer there. "One doesn't remember. One doesn't remember."

"Come on. Come on, tell me. What do you do to
them? Was it like that time in Buenos Aires? You
remember *that* one, don't you? That politician and his
mistress, that time you caught them in bed together and
it was supposed to look like a jealousy murder and a
suicide only you went too far and nobody would believe
it and they had to get you out of town in a hurry?
Don't tell me you didn't like touching *her*. Don't tell
me *she* didn't attract you. Was it like that last night,
Moreno? *Did she have anything on?*"

"It wasn't like that. Not like that. No, not like that.
Nothing on. Not attractive, no. Not like that."

"Well, what about me, then? Don't *I* attract you?"

Moreno's eyes moved slowly round towards her. Her
mouth was twisted slightly, as though in pain; she
loosened her bathrobe at the neck as he watched her,
touched the creamy skin at the base of her throat with
her silvertipped fingers; she saw his eyes follow the
movement, then turn as though reluctantly a little
farther downwards. There was a second of utter stillness; then he clapped one hand over his mouth as if
about to vomit, lurched to his feet and stood doubled
up over the table, staring down into the half-empty
milk-jug. Then, jerkily but very fast like a badly-
managed puppet, he threw himself round the table and
towards her. The handbag slithered down from her lap
and the Luger pistol raised its ugly black nozzle from
alongside her thigh to peer wickedly at Moreno's belly;
he stopped dead for a moment, brows lowered in a
frown of sudden perplexity, and in that moment they
both heard the click of the closing door. Then Feramontov's voice. "Put it down, Elsa. *Put it down.*"

Sunlight trembled along the full length of the blued-steel barrel. Then Elsa's fingers relaxed; the pistol turned downwards, lay once more on the blue flannel towelling of her bathrobe. Moreno's breath became suddenly audible in the silence, a succession of deep, shuddering gulps that shook his whole body; then he turned away, and Feramontov stepped aside to let him pass through the door. In his own expression there was something like a distant echo of Moreno's perplexity. He came slowly forward, hands dangling loosely at his sides.

"What exactly were you playing at?"

"He lost his temper," said Elsa. She laid the Luger down among the cups and plates on the snowy table-cloth, where it looked highly incongruous.

"Yes, he did. *That* wouldn't have stopped him, you know."

"Oh, yes, it would," said Elsa.

"You'd have killed him?"

"Rather than be killed . . . yes, of course."

"You were deliberately provoking him," said Feramontov. He made a statement of it, not a question.

"Not provoking him. Testing him."

"Testing him?"

"To see if, mentally, he was as unstable as I suspected. A man as unbalanced as he is . . . To my mind, he puts all the rest of us in danger."

Feramontov sat down. "If you don't mind my saying so, any such decision is not for you to make. Moreno is being employed by us on Head Office's recommendation. I assume you're not calling into question Head Office's competence to determine such matters?"

Elsa shrugged; adjusted the folds of her collar, which

the movement had disarranged. "Decisions also have to
be taken in the field."

"Sometimes. After previous consultation with the
executive. I don't remember your approaching me on
the subject."

"Like Moreno, I don't believe in wasting time."

"I certainly wouldn't have encouraged you in that
particular experiment. Moreno may, as you say, have
his little psychological failings. Why you should choose
to exacerbate them by a vulgar exploitation of sensuality, I can't imagine. You don't normally make a
practice of wearing a bathrobe with nothing underneath
it."

He reached out casually and jerked the bathrobe
open; then hit her equally casually, first with the palm
and then with the back of his hand. "In fact I object in
principle to your displaying your body to anyone other
than myself."

Elsa sat very still now, without looking at him and
without moving, making no attempt either to touch her
cheeks or to pull back the bathrobe over her breasts.
The impact of the blows had brought tears to her eyes;
otherwise, her expression was quite unaltered.
"Moreno's company seems to have had some effect
upon you. A pity."

"A gentle reminder, that's all, as to who is the boss."

"But hardly convincing."

"No?" He reached out his hand, unhurriedly as
before, and traced with the ball of his thumb a slow and
deliberate line round the full contour of her breast from
cleft to nipple. "Just how *does* one convince you?"

"I know too much about you to be convinced.
Herrgott in Himmel," said Elsa, in a sudden fury of

disgust. "*Ja, ein kleiner Casar—fur die Damen ein Mann und fur die Manner eine Frau.* Do you think that no one's *told* me anything about you? Or do you suppose I've been pawed round so much I just don't *care* any more? That last bit might be true—but there *are* limits."

"Indeed," said Feramontov, and pulled the bathrobe violently down from her shoulders. Elsa gave a little sigh, leaned forward and chopped with the heel of her hand at his throat; then stood up, pulling the bathrobe about her once more. Feramontov was on his knees, clawing at his shirt collar; in a few moments the blue tinge faded from his face and he stared up at her, his breath still rushing through to his lungs in painful jerks. Expressionless; quite expressionless. "A mistake," he said. "A serious mistake."

"Yours? Or mine?"

"Well. Both at fault. Perhaps." He got up, dusting punctiliously at his trousers. "Go to your room now, Elsa. Stay there. I'll talk to you later."

Elsa picked up her handbag, slipped the Luger into it; then left the room. Feramontov stood where he was, his head lowered, breathing slowly and regularly through his nose. Warm air drifted through the porthole, lifted the tiny hairs at the back of his neck; the soft salt-laden air of the Mediterranean. After a while he raised his head, stared at the clock on the imitation mantelpiece to his left. Then, rubbing his neck thoughtfully, he too turned and went out. The steward entered and, whistling, began to clear the breakfast table.

"COFFEE?" said Valera. "Why, yes. With a touch of milk, please. *Muy amable.*"

Fedora picked up the coffee-pot and poured.

Yesterday's newspaper, folded at the report of Moreno's escape, lay on the table a couple of feet from Valera's elbow. Valera had certainly noticed it, but as yet he hadn't commented on it; for twelve minutes he had done nothing but discuss the general circumstances attendant on Carmen's murder, and Moreno had so far not been mentioned. Fedora's patience was not exactly wearing thin, but he was now beginning to wonder if his idea of waiting for the police to make the first move had not been misconceived. The truth was that he had not expected an opponent quite so formidable as Valera. Few Spaniards can play a waiting game with any degree of success, but it was already amply clear that Valera was one of the few. Every one of Fedora's careful gambits had so far been neatly repulsed, and unless Valera now took the initiative the game seemed certain to end in stalemate. . . . A result that, from Johnny's viewpoint, would be unsatisfactory.

The truth was, of course, that Johnny needed to know a lot more about Moreno. What he knew of Moreno he knew from hearsay and from vague recollections of office files. A successful double agent in the last war, an operative of Soviet Intelligence afterwards in South America; a highly efficient intriguer in that branch of

international relations whose principal weapons are
slander and murder; a brilliant executive, a dangerous
psychopath, the High Executioner of the Soviet organisation overseas. In short, the nearest thing Russia had
to Fedora himself. Eight years back, he had been caught
and jailed on a faked-up charge by Franco's secret
police; that had counted as their greatest triumph since
the Civil War. Well, and now that he had escaped,
nothing seemed more natural than that the Russians
should have been waiting for him . . . should even have
helped to organise the break. . . . Political prisoners,
alone and unaided, hardly ever escaped from Spanish
prisons; Moreno was unique, of course, but even he
could hardly have achieved the impossible. . . .

"Sugar?" asked Johnny, politely.

"What? Oh yes. Yes, two lumps, if you please."

Big game, thought Fedora. The biggest of all. But he
wasn't alone in the hunt; that was the trouble. He had
certain advantages, but Valera had others. Such a trail
as he had to follow was anything but certain; the links
between El Anteojo and the *Polarlys* were very tenuous.
Chisels, diving-masks, the element of coincidence. In
themselves, they'd hardly be sufficient. But Fedora had an
instinct that served him when the hard facts failed, in which
at times he was prepared to rely completely. An instinct
about people such as Elsa, such as Valera, above all about
people such as the big dark-haired man he'd met aboard
the yacht. A man he hadn't been introduced to; who
didn't, perhaps, fit as perfectly as the others into the
simple preconceived plan of a scientific expedition. . . .

"You seem to be deep in thought, Sr. Fedora. If you
have any theories about the case, I should be interested
to hear them."

Johnny looked up. "Why?"

"I believe that the opinions of the man on the spot are always worth having."

"I wasn't thinking about the case, exactly. I was wondering, more, exactly what aspect of it could make it of interest to a member of the secret police."

"Ah, well, now," said Valera, and shook his index finger from side to side almost playfully. "That'd be telling, wouldn't it?"

He chuckled to himself and drank some more coffee. He was feeling fairly confident, because he now knew what the judge had meant when he had said that Fedora had been angry inside; Fedora, he could see, was angry still. Nothing showed in his face or in his posture, but the anger was emanating from him as heat from a radiator or cold from a block of ice. The latter was the better comparison, though. Because Fedora's anger was a cold anger, a freezing anger, a kind of controlled and creeping deadliness; something like the kind of anger that Acuña had shown on hearing of Juan Guerrero's death. And although there was nothing of impatience about it, Valera knew that by some small degree that anger would make his task easier for him; he could, if it came to the point, sit Fedora out; obtain what he needed to know with a minimum of concessions. Already, of course, he knew what formerly he had only guessed—that Fedora had somehow divined who had done the murder: that open newspaper could have no other explanation; it was a hint, an invitation to discussion, and Valera appreciated the subtlety of it. The present position, however, left him no room for subtleties. Subtleties were Acuña's stock-in-trade; as an executive officer, Valera had to approach such Gordian knots with a naked sword. A pity, in some ways. But there it was.

"I understand," he said, "that you yourself have some experience of Intelligence work. And so you can appreciate my problem. Normally, one bargains only with equals. Otherwise, of course, one stands to lose."

Fedora watched him closely, relaxed and yet not quite relaxed, one brown hand resting lightly on the tablecloth. "Bargains?" he repeated. His voice was gentle.

"In Intelligence work, information is often a great deal more valuable than money."

Fedora nodded. He understood. "Yes, that's true. Sometimes it can only be bought with other information."

"Although sometimes a price is offered that is very reasonable."

"Strange, isn't it?" said Fedora, and smiled. So did Valera.

"You speak and understand Spanish very well, Sr. Fedora. It's a pleasure to meet a foreigner who manages our language so skilfully. Even though, according to our files, you're not quite a foreigner. Your father was of Spanish origin, I believe?"

"That's right," said Johnny. "He was killed in the Civil War."

"Quite so. You would not, I suppose, have a grudge against the Spanish police on that account?"

"It happened a long time ago."

"That is our attitude, precisely. Nowadays we rarely bother people who have . . . let's say unfortunate political relationships dating from that unhappy period. I shouldn't like to feel that any such factor might be hindering our speaking frankly to one another."

"Although," said Johnny, "it must be difficult for you to consider such people as . . . equals."

"I see you follow me perfectly, Sr. Fedora."

"Perfectly. And that being the case," said Johnny, "I see no reason why—whatever happens—there should be any hard feelings between us, either way."

"Nothing but feelings of mutual respect."

"Some more coffee?"

"No, thank you. I must be going. I must make an early report to my superior." Valera got up from the table, bowed infinitesimally from the waist. "I have also to conduct an interview or two aboard the *Polarlys*. Alibis, after all, must be confirmed. A matter of routine, of course—we can't very well hold up their harbour clearance for more than an hour or two, and I gather they are anxious to be away." He picked up his hat, placed it tenderly upon his head and, no less tenderly, smiled in Fedora's direction. "I'm sure I shall be seeing you again very shortly."

He nodded pleasantly to Trout, who was sitting in the armchair by the window fanning himself with a paperbacked novel; then to Fedora. "Please don't trouble to see me out."

"No trouble," said Fedora.

Trout heard them go out into the hall, then the front door open and close. He sat up, dropping his Penguin into his lap, and drummed with his fingers on the arm of the chair. After a short pause, Fedora came back.

"You bit off a bit more than you could chew there, Johnny."

Fedora was sucking the back of his hand abstractedly. "I know," he said indistinctly. "It's a bastard."

"They know more than you thought they did. It even sounds as though they know about the *Polarlys*. No wonder it's no deal."

"Damn it," said Johnny. "Yes, but . . . damn it. We can't just let them hang us out to dry like *that*."

"You heard what he said. About as polite a threat as ever I've heard, but that's what it was. If you don't come across with what you know, he'll have you jugged. He'd *do* it, too. He's got all the cards."

"He knows more than we do, all right," said Johnny, sitting down once more at the table; even at that moment of stress, his actions were remarkably composed. "All the same, we must know something that *he* doesn't. Or he wouldn't bother about us at all."

"Or he may just *think* we know something he doesn't. I mean—he knows so much he may even have *expected* it."

"Expected what?"

"Expected Moreno to come here and collect whatever it was he *did* collect. Maybe the police even *let* him escape. To give him a chance to. . . . See what I'm getting at?"

Fedora took his knuckles out of his mouth and stared at Trout. "My God, Tiddler. That's bloody nearly bright of you."

"Well, and then, don't you see, he'd wonder what the hell *we* were doing here. Two ex-operatives of British Intelligence. . . . He just wouldn't believe it could be coincidence. We wouldn't in his place, would we? It looks as if we were camped down here waiting for it to happen."

"That puts us in a spot," said Johnny. "One hell of a spot."

"We *are* in a spot."

"If you're right."

"I *am* right. Don't you think so?"

"It makes solid sense from the ground up. No wonder he wouldn't play dicey."

"We have to get out of here," said Trout. "Or he'll jug us for sure. Even if we tell the truth now, he may not believe it."

Fedora got up abruptly, walked quickly over to the piano-stool. "Don't start playing *now*," said Trout, with some show of irritation. "I mean, this thing's getting serious. We have to do some fast thinking."

Johnny shrugged and began to play, the notes forming themselves slowly, like rising bubbles, under his fingers. "I know it's getting serious. He hasn't gone away."

"Gone away?"

"Valera hasn't. The car hasn't driven off. He's sitting in it, he's talking to his superior like he said—on the telephone. Ten to one says he's getting official approval for a precautionary arrest."

Trout got to his feet; turned towards the window, then back to Fedora. "And what are *we* going to do? Just sit here?"

"*I*'m going to sit here. While he hears the piano, he'll think we're both still here. Go on, Tiddler. Get moving."

Trout looked disgusted. "What's this? Heroics, at *your* time of life? Get off that burning deck, Casabianca."

"Oh balls," said Fedora, looking up savagely. "I don't have to *tell* you, do I? This is something that Macfarlane at Gib. ought to know about—you've got to get there and pretty damned quick. *He*'ll know what it is Moreno got out of that blasted pool; maybe he'll be in time to do something about it and maybe he won't, it all depends on you. It's only an hour to Gib. if you squeeze on the gas; you ought to get fifteen minutes' start on Valera and that'll have to be enough. Go on. Get moving."

"What about you?"

"Oh, me. It may be for years and it may be for ever. But this thing is bigger than both of us. Get moving, will you?"

"I hope to hell it is," said Trout, going to the side door. "That's all."

The door closed behind him. Fedora bent down over the keyboard, settling down with studious determination on one of the more imposing passages from the first movement of the *Emperor*. Wonderful music, that; wonderfully *loud*. Loud enough, perhaps, to mask the sound of a car starting up a hundred yards away behind the house. At any rate, Fedora hoped so. He bounced his hands vindictively up and down on the keys, banging out great rolling chords with bags of *sostenuto*, real Gieseking stuff. Drops of sweat began to gather on his forehead. . . .

VALERA was talking to his superior, but not on the telephone. Johnny had, in part, underestimated Acuña; Acuña was in the car. Acuña, in fact, was the driver. He sat slumped at the steering-wheel with his grey cotton jacket unbuttoned at the neck and a brown-paper cigarette, stained with saliva, dangling nonchalantly from the corner of his mouth; indistinguishable in outward appearance from any other disillusioned *chofer madrileño*. He listened with an air of refined boredom to what Valera was saying, leaning forward once to spit with commendable accuracy out of the window. "You seem," he said in the end, "to have concentrated rather exclusively on Fedora."

"He did all the talking. He's the one who speaks Spanish the best, of course."

"I can't say I like the situation."

"At least, up to a point, we retain command of it. He made it clear that he wanted to trade information, and that shows that as yet he doesn't know enough to make any kind of a move."

"Yes. But now you've told him we're not interested in that kind of a deal, he's almost bound to make some kind of a move anyway. We don't want that. He's got one thing, at least, that we haven't."

"What's that?"

"Bait."

"Bait?"

"Yes. He's got the one bait that Moreno can scent a mile off—the one thing that'll bring him running. He mustn't be allowed to use it, that's all."

Valera frowned. "I don't quite know what bait you mean."

"Himself."

"Ahhhh! *Ya comprendo*," said Valera.

"Those two are about the top of the tree at their business—but on opposite sides. They hate each other's guts by the purest instinct. You saw that much for yourself. You know the English saying about the cats of Kilkenny?"

"No."

"They fight whenever and wherever they meet. That's all."

Valera considered for a moment. "There's only one way to stop him using that bait, of course."

"Precisely. That's why I approve the step you were going to suggest."

"Both of them?"

"Of course." Acuña took the cigarette-stub from his mouth and tossed it out the window. "Treat them with every consideration, mind you. If they decide to co-operate, it'll make our task that much easier."

Valera nodded. "And the *Polarlys*?"

"What about the *Polarlys*?"

"I think our guess about that may have been a good one. I mentioned it just before I left, to see if there was any reaction."

"And was there?"

"No. You wouldn't expect it, would you?—from someone of Fedora's class. All the same, I'm prepared to back my instinct."

"How far?"

"All the way."

"You think Moreno's on board?"

"I'm almost sure of it."

"And Feramontov?"

"Probably."

"Moreno and Feramontov. Yes, I know what you're thinking. It'd be a wonderful haul." Acuña sighed windily. "But we can't do it. We have to play for safety. It's fatal to change objectives halfway through an operation. You know that as well as I do."

"What do you advise, then?"

"I agree that we ought to make some move. But not towards Moreno. Not towards Feramontov, either. Strike at the weakest link, that's the golden rule."

"Yes, sir." Valera lit a cigarette, waited patiently.

"I've been checking with the harbour authorities. They have a woman aboard; rather an attractive woman, too, if her photograph's anything to go by. She's the one you want. Take her in. Women are a weakness in any organisation; the Reds know that perfectly well, yet they *will* go on using them—I suppose in support of their political theories. It's odd."

"They're not particularly weak when it comes to talking. I'd say they were tougher than men, taken by and large."

"Yes, yes. No doubt. Well, you'll naturally put her on the grid as a matter of course, and if she *does* talk, so much the better. But that's not the main idea. The main idea is simply to get them rattled. You'd be surprised if you knew how much dissension a woman can cause, and if we can get them thinking in two different ways . . . well, they'll be a whole lot more likely to make a mistake. Even Feramontov won't find it easy to handle a paranoid like Moreno, where there's a woman in the case. So that's what we'll do. Hold up their clearance papers for a few hours on some technicality or other, just to get them worried. Then weigh in and grab the girl. We'll see what happens."

"Any special grounds?"

Acuña's expression became distant, his eyes faintly glazed. Valera knew that he had no more to say on the subject. "All right, sir," he said, opening the car door. "I'll rope the Englishmen in right away, just to be on the safe side. And then I'll get moving."

Acuña was now listening, his head cocked a little to one side and a half-smile on his face. "He plays the piano damned well," he said. "He almost deserves to get away with it."

Valera stopped, one foot on the gravel. "To get away with what?"

"I've only just realised," said Acuña. "Go on, Captain. You'll soon see with what."

Valera marched up to the front door once more, pressed his finger on the doorbell. Inside, the swelling succession of chords slowed down infinitesimally, then ceased; and there was silence. Valera waited some thirty seconds, then tried again. Still nothing happened. He took the pistol from his shoulder holster, walked quickly round to the french window. Fedora stood there, just inside the room, smoking a cigarette.

"So there you are," he said. "Come on in."

FERAMONTOV came quickly into Elsa's cabin, closing the door behind him. Elsa was sitting cross-legged on the table, putting fresh varnish on her finger-nails. . . . "What," he asked, "have you been up to?"

"Nothing," said Elsa. She shrugged. "Other than what I was told. I've been here all morning."

"There's two Civil Guards just come aboard. They want to speak to you."

"What about?"

"Don't be irritating. How should *I* know what about?"

"Perhaps the best thing would be for me to see them. That way, we can find out."

"Don't be facetious, either. I repeat, what have you been up to? Meuvret's just found out that our clearance certificate is being delayed for some reason. And I don't believe in coincidences, as I've said before." He took her chin in his hand, twisted it round until she was facing him. "You haven't done anything really *stupid*, have you Elsa?"

"You seemed to think so, this morning."

"That business was stupid enough, of course. But it wasn't what I meant. And you know it."

Elsa said, "Have you any reason not to trust me?"

"No," said Feramontov. "Not as yet. But I haven't any special reason for trusting you, either."

Elsa closed her eyes. "I apologise. Such an obscene expression, isn't it."

"Obscene, no. But meaningless, unless carefully used. I should like to think that you were a careful person, Elsa, and that you intend to be particularly careful now."

"You know that I'm careful."

"I've always believed so," said Feramontov.

He increased the pressure of his thumb against the edge of her chin, tilting her head upwards; her eyes came suddenly open, her lips apart. She made no attempt to move away as he brought his mouth slowly down on hers, but bit instead deep into his lower lip; he gasped, jerked himself away. "*A vi, a vi,*" he said between his teeth. "*Poslushayte, Elsa—*"

"Let me alone. That's all."

He wiped his mouth with the back of his hand and stared down bemusedly at the blood on his knuckles. He looked like Raskolnikov, thought Elsa, after the murder; and she was instantly almost alarmed by the inconsequence of this idea. His having spoken for once in Russian, that might have been the cause . . . but even so. . . . She twisted herself away from the table, balancing herself on the balls of her feet. For a moment she and Feramontov looked at one another, and she knew that this time she was genuinely frightened of him. And as she knew very little of fear, she found the sensation doubly unpleasant.

Even so, it was Feramontov who looked away; to take a handkerchief from his pocket and apply it to his puffed-up lip. "Very well," he said. "Very well. You had better go and see the gentlemen of the Civil Guard. Unless you wish to . . . compose yourself first."

"Thank you," said Elsa. "I'm quite composed."

She drew the sash of the bathrobe tighter round her

waist and moved towards the door. Feramontov's
yellowish feline eyes watched her all the way. "You're
going like that?"

"Like what?"

"Wearing a bathrobe?"

"And nothing else. Exactly."

"I thought I'd made it clear—"

"Oh, shut up," said Elsa, and went out.

She was probably in the wrong, though, and she
knew it. It would hardly create a favourable impression.
The truth was that she *wasn't* quite composed, not yet;
otherwise she would certainly have stopped to change.
Now it was too late; the gesture had been made and a
silly one it had been, but there it was. Feramontov's
fault. . . .

She felt a moment of despairing hatred, as she walked
down the narrow corridor, for Feramontov and for all men;
trouble, always trouble. There had been a certain pleasure, of course, in inflicting upon him that painful and
summary defeat; even perhaps a certain pleasure in that
brief contact of their mouths; her lips still felt bruised from
that first fierce pressure, tingled with a dry heat. A
fruitless, meaningless pleasure, though. It made no sense.

Like the pleasure one gets from the knowledge that
one's body is beautiful, that its beauty confers a certain
dangerous power. Elsa had used her body in that way
often enough not to underestimate its value as a
practical asset to the Party and more directly to herself
. . . and perhaps too often, since now she felt as much
scorn for those who succumbed to the power of her body
as for those who sought to profit by it. What made
Feramontov intolerable was simply the fact that he
should try to do both.

Well, and what was the use of a lovely body if it brought no other pleasures than those? Power by itself could not be enough; it left no resort but to misuse it, as perhaps she had done with Moreno. Beauty is a blade with two edges. That, maybe, was why Feramontov couldn't trust her. She had brains as well, of course. But that only made it worse.

She hesitated for a moment outside the white-painted door of the dining-room, then went on through. The Civil Guards were standing by the table, their shiny black hats in their hands, uniforms smartly creased. They turned as she came in, and looked towards her. They were men. She hated them, too.

"WELL, we've arrested her," said the District Judge. "And you've got half the local police force at your disposal, should you feel like arresting anyone else. Just let me know. That's all."

He sounded rather bitter, thought Valera. Probably the girl had put up a fuss; it was surprising, in a way, how Spanish officials hated the very sound of the word *Consulate*. "That's fine," he said. "I'm very much obliged to you. You know where to send her?"

"She's on the way now. Under escort."

"That's fine," said Valera again. He put down the telephone. The first part of the programme, then, had gone off without a hitch. Or *almost* without a hitch. He stared sourly at Fedora, who was sitting with one leg slung casually over the arm of a chair reading the morning's newspaper; then walked over to the window, gazed out for a while on a particularly bleak and inhospitable stretch of the sierra, dotted with jagged boulders. He knew that this house was called the Finca de los Tresillistas and he could see that it had once formed part of some not very prosperous farm; and this was the sum extent of his knowledge. Not that he was worried by this; he was thoroughly accustomed to operating from improvised headquarters, ramshackle buildings he had never seen before and heartily hoped never to see again; this one had at least the advantages of silence and privacy. The surroundings were so quiet that he could hear the rattle of a typewriter coming from the next room but one; his secretary was knocking out a draft report. Valera hated reports. They were necessary, but necessary evils. Frowning slightly, he walked back to the chair by the telephone and, gracefully hitching up his trousers, sat down.

"Comfortable, Sr. Fedora?"

Johnny lowered the newspaper a fraction, looked at him over the top of it. "Well, no. Not really."

"It's rather a change from El Anteojo, I'll admit. Temporary headquarters are hardly ever palatial." He took a black cigar from his breast pocket, bit the end off reflectively. "However, we propose to treat you with every consideration. You'll realise that in the ordinary way we'd lean backwards to avoid arresting you. Unfortunately, the present situation calls for extraordinary measures."

Johnny smiled. "I don't like extraordinary measures. They're so much easier to predict than the other kind."

"*Touché.* But what precisely is *your* prediction, Sr. Fedora? What course, in the present situation, would *you* adopt?"

"I don't know what the present situation is. But from what I know of the Secret Police—in Spain, and generally—I think I could risk a prediction in any case."

". . . Go on."

"Just follow the golden rule," said Johnny. "When in doubt, hurt someone."

Valera's grey eyes swivelled briefly in Johnny's direction; he struck a match on the wall to his right, lit the cigar. "Commendably accurate," he said. "But hurt who? *You*, for instance?"

"Oh no. I don't think so."

"Why not?"

"You're still hoping that, if you play things right, I'll work along with you. And you're pretty sure that what I know isn't worth the trouble it'd take to get it out of me. You're right, incidentally. I've been known to be obstinate."

Valera nodded. "Yes. I've seen your file. And we don't pretend to be more efficient in these matters than the Gestapo used to be. All the same, our methods aren't to be despised. And as you're something of an expert, I wouldn't mind having your opinion of them."

He blew out smoke, fanned it away with the flat of his hand. Fedora looked down at the newspaper, folded it, laid it down on the table. ". . . Who?" he said, suddenly.

"The girl from the yacht."

"I see," said Johnny. He thought for a moment, then shrugged. "I wouldn't be over-confident."

"You think she, too, will be obstinate?"

"Very obstinate."

"You, of course, have met the lady. I haven't, as yet. But I understand that physically she's attractive."

"That doesn't always help."

"It didn't always help the Gestapo. But this girl isn't one of your admirable Resistance fighters, Sr. Fedora. She's a German, working for the Russians. *They* don't trust the pretty ones, you know. And the girls know it. Nothing weakens the morale so much as the lack of mutual trust. It may take some time, of course, but I fancy that in the end she'll talk." Valera looked pensively at the glowing end of his cigar, fingered away the loose ash. "In any case, when they're pretty . . . it makes the work a little more pleasant."

"So it *is* the Russians," said Johnny. "I wondered."

"Ah, come now," said Valera. "That much at least you must have known."

Fedora pushed out his lower lip, sank his chin down on to his chest. *Extraordinary measures*, he thought; yes, but how very unextraordinary they always are, they're the oldest measures of all. In Russia, in Spain, in China, in America; always the same old game. *When in doubt.* . . . And this time it was going to be Elsa. Valera's voice, flat, unemotional; *I understand that physically she's attractive*. Yes, she's attractive all right. She's attractive now. But for how much longer? A woman's body is made of flesh; flesh can be creased, can be burnt, can be twisted and scarred. . . .

He lifted his head, stared—as Valera had done—out of the window towards the high sierra. Grey rocks, the grey hillside, a deep blue sky. But what he saw was the palely-shining floor of the pool, twelve, fifteen feet under water, and the long dark shape, like a fish and yet not like a fish, that nosed at the walls at the bottom. Then the sound of bare feet on a gravel path, of a girl humming quietly to herself; then the splash, the sputter of white foam, the clean arc traced by her limbs in the water. And the shape beneath her turning suddenly yet smoothly, like a hunting shark, rising with ominous speed to meet her; two figures merging in an unexpected and violent embrace; then the limp body and the wide circles of blood on the pool's dimpled surface, the dark masked shape vanishing again into the depths. The oldest measures of all; an eye for an eye, a tooth for a tooth; the rough tribal justice that civilised men still recognised and found appropriate. Elsa and Carmen would at last be joined together in the final democracy of pain. . . .

He saw the girl coming up the pathway that ran
through the rocks, walking between two Civil Guards,
her head black and gleaming in the noonday sunlight,
as black as their shiny black hats. She wore a bathrobe
of dark blue towelling, under which her legs were bare
and brown; her hands were pushed deep into her
pockets. He took out a handkerchief, carefully wiped
the perspiration from his neck and forehead.

It was a very hot day.

". . . For being indecently dressed?" said Feramontov.
"I don't believe it. Look, I'm damned if I'll believe it."

"They said there'd been complaints about that
bathing dress of hers," said Meuvret. "Don't ask me
why. It *could* be true. Then, of course, she showed up
wearing that bathrobe of hers which doesn't even cover
her *knees* and what's more, it didn't look as though she
was wearing—"

"I don't believe it. Who do they think I am? Who
does *she* think I am? She's bloody well defected, that's
what." Feramontov's fingers caressed his swollen lower
lip, adorned now by a strip of sticking-plaster. "That's
why they're holding up the clearance certificate. That
by itself needn't have meant anything—that could have
just been the usual blasted Spanish lazy-mindedness—
but taken in with the other, it can't be accident. I just
don't believe it."

"I wouldn't have thought she'd defect. Not a girl
with Elsa's record."

"I'm not so sure. She's been behaving damned oddly
lately." Aware of Meuvret's gaze, Feramontov took
his hand away from his lip a little too abruptly. "Any-

way, I'm not taking any chances—not now. It's too late for that. If we're not cleared by five o'clock, we'll leave anyway. And be damned to them."

"And Elsa?"

"Bruniev'll look after that side of things. That's what he's there for. Besides, it'll make for a useful diversion just when we need it. Send the radio operator to see me at once."

"At once," echoed Meuvret. He turned towards the door.

"Oh, and Meuvret. . . . "

". . . Yes?"

". . . Don't tell Moreno."

VALERA was a good interrogator. He had studied the books and the methods. The Communist, the Chinese, the Gestapo, the F.B.I.—he knew them all. He was careful, conscientious, and—unlike most Spaniards—very patient. He passed the heat of the afternoon in his room, taking a siesta; he had had very little sleep the night before, and he believed in starting fresh. At half-past-four exactly, he called his secretary; and the interrogation began.

Fedora came down some forty-five minutes later to watch him at work. It was a small room, and stifling hot; Valera sat in a cane chair with his tie loose and his collar unbuttoned, his white shirt stained with sweat beneath the armpits, and behind him sat his secretary, impassive, motionless, with a shorthand notebook open on her lap. One of the Civil Guards stood by the door, right hand on his revolver holster, looking straight in front of him at the far wall. And the girl sat stiffly upright in a chair in the centre of the room, her wrists and ankles strapped tightly against the hard wood; her head had fallen sideways and the light from the angled lamp beat fiercely against her glossy black hair. Valera nodded to Johnny in the abstracted way of an eminent businessman engrossed in his work.

"Much as we expected," he said.

"Nothing?"

"Nothing that matters. They're well-taught, you

know." Then, as though he felt the excuse to be unsatisfactory, "These things take a little time."

"I see. Do you always take their clothes off?"

"Well, usually. It lowers a woman's resistance, you know. Or at least, it's supposed to." His voice sounded too dry, almost hoarse. "Not the Commies, though. They know what to expect. Why, she wasn't wearing anything anyway, except for a bathrobe. Cheek enough for six."

That's how Carmen ended up, thought Johnny. ". . . An eye for an eye."

"What?"

"Nothing. Just something I was thinking."

". . . You don't approve?"

"It makes me feel a bit uncomfortable."

"So it did me, at first. You get used to it," said Valera gruffly. "Don't you do it this way in England?"

Fedora looked towards the painfully rigid figure in the chair, at the long lines of angry cigarette-burns on its naked arms and shoulders. "No," he said. "If they keep their clothes, it makes them more face-conscious. It's the face they mind the most, usually. . . . "

He stopped abruptly. *Think of the pool,* he said to himself, *of the turning shark, the blood spouting red to the surface. An eye for an eye. Extraordinary measures. . . .*

"Interesting," said Valera. "Myself, I prefer to work round to the face by degrees. I'm not impatient. I don't worry. *She* knows." He began to roll a cigarette with an air of quiet satisfaction. There was a sharp rap on the door; the Civil Guard opened it, then came across to Valera with a written message in his hand. Valera took it, glanced at it briefly. "Telephone call," he said. "Ah well. Lucky I was taking a break anyhow." He got up.

". . . You want to carry on?"

"I'm fresh out of cigarettes," said Fedora.

"What? Oh, *that*. No, she takes that as though it were sunburn. Just talk to her, that's all. Take her through her words all over again, right from the beginning. It tires them, you know. They get cross. And besides, you're old friends, aren't you?" He looked back from the door and winked prodigiously. "You wanted information, didn't you? Well, now's your chance."

He walked off down the corridor; the Civil Guard closed the door after him, and with the same movement drew his revolver from its holster. Yes, all very friendly, thought Fedora; but they're playing it safe for all that. Not that one can blame them. He sat down heavily in the cane chair, his knees within a yard of Elsa's. At that distance he could detect the pungent smell of burnt skin, mingling with a stronger, salty smell like that of the sea and with the remnants of a dab of *Vent Vert*. It was curious that she wasn't yet afraid. Fear has a smell that is all its own; unmistakable. Fedora hated it.

After a while, her head came up and she looked at him. Her eyes were utterly devoid of thought: they seemed to see him not as a man but as part of the furniture; she sat as though drugged by the remembrance of pain. All the same, she knew who he was. ". . . Tell me about Moreno," he said. Her eyes remained unwaveringly in focus on his face. It was like talking to a wall, except in that something behind the eyes was almost frighteningly human. More than human. Feminine. ". . . Elsa," Fedora said. "Tell me about Moreno."

Her lips opened, moved. ". . . Surprise."

"What?" He leaned forward.

". . . Surprise to see you here."

"Yes. Yes, I suppose it must be."

"British Intelligence. We live and learn. I suppose you knew." Not all the words were coming out; Johnny could see her making a conscious effort to speak clearly, as a drunken man might. "No, but you couldn't have. You wouldn't have let him do it."

"Who? Moreno?"

Something came down to curtain off whatever expression there had been behind her eyes; she looked down at the floor. *Da⁝n,* thought Fedora. *I had a chance there.* He let his hands relax, curl up in his lap. "Would you like to get dressed?"

Again her lips moved for a moment before she spoke. "I've only got a bathing-robe. It doesn't make much difference." A pause, then, ". . . I'm sorry if it makes you feel uncomfortable."

"Did you hear me say that?"

"Of course."

"You heard it all, did you?" *Well, then she must think I'm working in with Valera. Obviously she must. Yes, I've gone and underestimated Valera again. He's a clever basket.* "I thought you were taking a nap."

She looked up at him again. "One rests when one is allowed to," she said. "I don't think I'm particularly afraid. I'm not 'face-conscious', as you put it. We'll continue as soon as you like."

Johnny shook his head. "I don't use those methods myself."

"You merely recommend them?"

"Moreno made a very thorough job of Carmen," said Johnny savagely. "And Carmen was my housemaid. And so I want Moreno. And you're in the way. Just what do you expect me to recommend? If you tangle with people like Moreno, you damned well deserve all you get."

He leaned forward, unbuckled the straps at her wrists and ankles. The Civil Guard took an anxious pace forward, stopped when the secretary raised her hand. "You can't hide any poison capsules in a bathrobe," said Fedora. "You may as well put it on again."

Elsa stood up, swayed, fell forward on to her hands and knees. Fedora made no attempt to catch her, though her face missed colliding with the arm of his chair by a matter of an inch. He looked down at her, curled up on the floor; at the dark cascade of her hair almost touching his shoes, at the rounded upward thrust of her raised hip and at the shadows beneath the tilt of her lifted breasts. In the chair, her nakedness had been evident and yet impersonal, untouchable; the suddenness with which, in falling to the floor, she had become entirely and provocatively a woman had taken him by surprise, had caught unexpectedly at his throat, leaving him with a nervous, quivering ache at the pit of his stomach. He watched her slowly recover, push herself up from the floor and regain her feet; his hands remained folded against his thighs, relaxed, unmoving. "Thank you," she said.

"What for?"

"For not touching me."

"I know how it is," said Johnny gently. "After this sort of a session, one isn't in the mood. I know. I've had some myself."

She stood in front of him beside the chair, her whole being concentrated on the simple act of staying on her feet. Fedora picked up the crumpled blue bathrobe from the floor, handed it to her; watched her as she struggled her way into it. She didn't wince, he noticed, when the rough material brushed the raw burns on her upper arms and shoulders; she was tough, all right. But that he had guessed from the first. ". . . There," she said, turning back towards him. "Perhaps now you'll feel more at ease."

Fedora smiled. "I doubt it," he said. "You were right. It doesn't make much difference."

She sat down again in the chair, crossing her legs with an attempted casualness that Johnny admired. "Now," he said. "Now tell me about Moreno."

"I don't know anyone called Moreno. Sorry."

"Then I'll tell *you* about him," said Fedora. He spoke heavily, but a little more evenly than before. "Moreno is a man who has killed four people in two days. Four *innocent* people, if that word means anything. He's clever but he's not normal. He's a psychopath. And whatever game it is that your people and our people are playing, he shouldn't be allowed any part in it. That's how *I* feel about him, anyway."

Elsa was watching him intently now. "Who *are* your people, exactly?"

"To tell the truth, I'm on my own in this. Let's say the Spaniards, then."

"Someone told me your father was a Spaniard."

"So he was."

"And your mother was English?"

"No. Irish."

"All the same, you have to be English." Elsa sighed. "Only the English ever talk of playing games."

"Just a way of putting it," said Johnny, "like any other."

"My parents were German Jews and the Nazis murdered them both. *That* wasn't a game."

"My parents were murdered, too," said Fedora. "By the Falangist police, in the Civil War. In a room probably not very different to this one."

A moment's silence. Then the girl said, with a certain contempt, "What sort of a man does that make *you*?"

"I sometimes wonder," said Johnny.

"I don't understand. You ought to be on our side. Not theirs."

The secretary coughed. Fedora looked round. He had almost forgotten about her. But there she was, her ball-point pen sliding silently over the pages of her notebook. "Our side? Their side?" he said, returning his attention to Elsa. "Now *you*'re talking as though it were a game. You haven't got a side, not any more. You've been arrested. That makes it just a matter of which of them gets you first. Hadn't you thought of that?"

"Yes. I had. I'd been thinking that it might be. . . . "

"Yes?" said Johnny. This time, he didn't lean forward.

". . . Moreno."

"WELL, it won't be Moreno," said Valera. "It won't be Moreno because the damned ship's sailed. Without a clearance. So we've put the wind up them anyway, which is what we were planning to do, and now I'm just hoping to hell we can keep a tag on them. Anyway, no need to worry about the other thing; we don't make a habit of losing our prisoners, once we've got them. Not her nor *you*, either . . . *Mister* Fedora."

THREE men were at that moment walking down Larios in Malaga. They had little in common, in so far as outward appearance went: two were middle-aged, while the third was aged about twenty and looked rather younger. One of the elder men wore a moustache and long Valentino sideburns; the other had bushy eyebrows and a mournful expression. All three were dressed in dark suits of more than ordinarily good quality, though the boy wore no tie.

They entered a bar at one side of the Avenida and talked for a while in low-pitched voices. They were all expert and conscientious workmen, and—although they had been well briefed already—certain points of detail remained to be ironed out amongst themselves. Their conversation lasted for perhaps twenty minutes. At the end of it, the boy got up and went out.

The other two men finished their beers and talked about boxing until a car drew up outside; then they, too, left the bar. The car was a Renault Dauphine, almost new but not especially noticeable. It carried a Sevilla numberplate. They climbed into the back and the boy at once drove off, turning sharp right to mount the bridge and take the Marbella road.

Nobody said anything further until they had passed Fuengirola village. Then, near the old castle, the car pulled into the side of the road and stopped. The boy got out, unloaded a heavy leather case from the boot.

He passed it through to the men in the back seat, went
back to the driving-seat and set the car going again.

The man with the bushy eyebrows opened the bag,
began to fit together the component parts of a Sten
machine carbine. The man with the moustache took
the grenades from the side pocket and primed them
carefully, later unbuttoning his jacket and clipping
them securely to his belt. The hands of both men moved
smoothly, automatically, with casual efficiency. They
were well-practised. Until two months ago, they had
been fighting against the French in Algeria; tonight
they had been given a new and different target, but
their methods would be much the same as always. The
car drove on, meanwhile, through the pine woods. The
men in the back seat lit cigarettes, and after a while the
interior of the car began to reek of the softly pungent
smell of marijuana.

The boy drove on without looking round. He didn't
need the help of hashish or of anything else. His name
was Mariano. He had melting brown eyes and steady
hands and he was good with both the pistol and the
knife. Moreover, he knew that he was good. He alone
of the three was something more than a conscientious
workman; he had pride. He smoked four cigarettes a
day, one after each meal; when, as sometimes happened,
he didn't eat, he didn't smoke either. He never drank
intoxicants and he never took drugs. He didn't much
like women. He was a good boy, was Mariano.

He was inclined to be contemptuous of his compan-
ions. He knew them hardly at all, but he knew well
enough the lines on which they would be thinking.
Their thoughts would always move in grooves, along
Party lines of military orthodoxy. Straightforward

textbook methods, tried and trusty; find, fix and strike; the sudden, irresistible application of violence to a chosen end, the unimaginative trial of strength. First the slow, cautious approach, localising the enemy; then the grenades in through the window—*one, two*—and the sharp sickening blasts; then the door kicked open, the quick unflustered dart to left or right, the staccato rattle of the tommy-gun, the room suddenly stinking of cordite, full of smoke, splattered with blood. . . . That was the military mind for you, thought Mariano scornfully. His own methods were rather different. Flitting from room to room as silently as a ghost, the four-inch blade flickering briefly with each noiseless thrust. No stabbing, no needless expenditure of energy; just slipping the blade into place, resting the arm's weight against it. A gasp, maybe, and a jerk; but that would be all. Discreet, effortless. Instead of that, Chicago stuff. Hand grenades, machine pistols, shouts, screams, bodies contorted in death. It would be *effective*, of course. The operation would be successful. But all so unnecessary. Mariano's upper lip curled slightly as he pushed the Renault up the final rise that took them into Marbella village; and he glanced once, quickly, down at his wristwatch. Half past eight, and twilight beginning to fall. Dead on time. He span the wheel, turned the car towards the hills, up the narrow road to Ojen.

They were talking now, the two on the back seat. He didn't bother to listen. He lifted his right hand from the wheel, twisted his fingers up towards his wrist and felt the tips touch the bone handle of the knife strapped to his forearm. The curl of his lips became happier. He drove on, listening absently to the whisper of the tyres on the dry asphalt. The mountains grew around him.

The men behind him became silent. Ten minutes later, he heard cloth rustle as the man with the moustache leaned forward.

"*Craches-nous ici, Mariano. Ici a la gauche.*"

"*D'ac,*" he said.

He let the car's speed die away slowly, as though he were strangling it. A space opened up between a pine clump and a patch of waste; he nosed the car into it, braked, cut off the lights. For a few more moments, everything was still. Then a man in grey oilstained trousers came from the trees to stand beside the car, stooping down to peer cautiously into the windows.

"From Malaga?"

"That's right," said the man with the moustache. "From Malaga."

"Good. She's still there."

"How many policemen?"

"Four. And two in plain clothes. And there's a woman—some kind of a secretary."

"Two in plain clothes. We know about *those*," said the man with the moustache. His Spanish was execrable, but fluent enough. "*Brigada Secreta. Cochinos, cabrónes.* How far away?"

"Maybe a kilometre. Just over the crest."

"All right. Let's go, then."

They got out of the car and looked around them. It was darker in the shadow of the mountains, and the early stars were out in the evening sky. All about them was a vast silence; the man with the bushy eyebrows moved uneasily from one foot to the other. "*C'est bien tranquille, merde, ici.*"

"*Oui. Sommes en banlieu, quoi?*" The man with the moustache patted gently at the bulges inside his jacket.

"We'll liven things up a bit before long. Come on, then. *Vamonos*."

The four of them moved off over the hard, warm earth, Mariano in the rear. He could smell the scent of the pine resin and of the distant sea; the shapes of great rocks formed about him as he walked, boulders like sleeping animals. At the top of the rise the land fell away to the right, and he saw quite near the lights of the farmhouse. They paused for a moment, then moved on again.

He took the pistol from its shoulder holster and worked the sleeve, pumping a round up into the firing chamber. The metal slid smoothly into place, the safety-catch went forward with a barely audible click. He held the pistol in his hand as they emerged from the boulders and came to a halt in the shadows, the building now no more than a hundred yards away.

The man in the dirty trousers raised his arm and pointed. "The woman's in that room with the grey curtains. Where that chink of light's coming out—you see? There's a cop on guard at the door. And there's two more playing cards there in the front. The other one's at the front door."

"Yes. I can see *him*. And the plain-clothes boys?"

"Most of the time they're in with *her*. But they keep moving about."

"They would," said the man with the moustache. "Okay. Hop it."

The other man turned and disappeared into the shadows. And the man with the moustache nodded to Mariano; who went forward over the dry grass. He moved fast, not bothering to crouch, but quietly and with caution. He reached the window at the back, the window next to the room with the grey curtains; laid the pistol on the sill. His hands worked stiffly with sticky tape, a glass-cutter: the window-catch came open, then the window itself. He braced himself for a moment, then vaulted up and into the dark gap.

The two elder men were now moving forward, too; towards the room where the two guards sat playing *siete-y-media*. Looking back through the window, Mariano saw them as fleeting dark figures coming up to spreadeagle themselves by the greyish-white walls of the farmhouse: this was to be too easy, he thought, a piece of cake. The cops hadn't any reason to expect this kind of attack. They'd be sitting at the table, close together, so that the grenades could go in at the same angle—one a shade shorter than the other, though, in case the table held too much of the blast. That, at least, was how *he* would have done it. . . .

Ah, but tonight he had his own job to do. And it was time to get on with it. He turned and moved away from the window, eyes wide-open like a cat's in the near-darkness, walking across the empty room towards the corridor. . . .

VALERA was actually walking down the corridor when he heard the angry blast of the grenades, the sudden jitter of the Sten gun. The echoes were still ringing in his ears as he kicked the door open and stepped into the guard-room; the air was full of dust, of flakes of plaster, the acrid after-tinge of high explosive. He jumped to his right without glancing towards the two crumpled figures by the shattered table, moving with surprising speed for a man of his bulk; the man at the window with a grenade in his hand swayed to follow the movement, and Valera shot him through the neck. His fingers clawed for a second at the sill, then he disappeared; a long two seconds later, the grenade exploded; the solid wall seemed to heave and the remnants of glass in the window dissolved into a hail of splinters. Valera dived for the front door and out into the courtyard, almost tripping over the body of the guard; one of the two men by the window was crawling towards him with infinite effort, his smashed legs dragging uselessly behind him; he tried to raise the Sten to his shoulder, and Valera shot him through the head. The other had received the full impact of the grenade and lay like a heap of old clothes; Valera stared at him for a second, then stepped back into the house. He was angry, more than angry; he was filled with unreasoning Spanish fury. "*Manolo!*" he bawled at the top of his voice, striding towards the corridor. "What the hell are you waiting for? They got Carlos, God damn it, they got the other two as well, they're starting a bloody *war* by the look of it. Get Fedora and the girl out of there—"

He stopped, staring down the passage. Manolo the Civil Guard lay on the red brick tiles at the far end, clutching his belly; blood trickled wetly through his fingers. Valera swore, raced down the passage towards the door that lay behind Manolo's shiny upturned boots; knowing, as he ran, that he was almost certainly too late. . . .

. . . Because the door was open. . . .

MARIANO—one death the more to his credit—stood balanced on the balls of his feet just inside the room; the woman with the notebook in her hand was screaming, so he shot her. It was a reflex action, hardly a conscious one. He watched as the heavy bullet span her sideways out of the chair to land in a heap by the wall, and his upper lip wrinkled back over his teeth—another reflex action, a sort of a smile, perhaps. The other two people in the room sat very still and did not move. There was a man in a biscuit-coloured cotton suit, thin-faced, blue-eyed; there was a girl in a blue bathing-wrap; the girl was the one he had come to kill and therefore should be the first. He turned the pistol casually in her direction, pressed the trigger; as he did so the tall man jerked out his leg and kicked the chair from under her, sprawling her to the floor in a sudden chaos of swirling cloth and long suntanned thighs. The bullet kicked plaster from the wall directly behind her; Mariano grimaced and stepped to one side, levelling the pistol for a second shot; and Valera came through the door full tilt and crashed straight into him.

The pistol scuttered over the floor as they went down together, Mariano underneath, and while he fell the knife was curving from his fingertips into his palm. His shoulders were tensing even as they struck the floor, driving the blade upwards; he felt the agonised outrush of Valera's breath on his face, the jerk of contracting muscles around the steel; then he was rolling clear of the weight of the other's body, the knife free again in his hand, was rolling clear and bouncing to his feet. The tall man was also on his feet now, watching him closely, his eyes pale blue, seemingly amused; Mariano's hand swivelled back to flick the knife delicately into his throat; and then something smashed like a ton of ice into the small of his back, breaking his spine like a twig, bowling him to the floor. In the second before he died—a second of preternaturally sharp vision in which a whole lost world of movement and colour unfolded like a flower and vanished—he saw the girl kneeling in the corner with his pistol in her hand, saw the brown eyes wide open behind the barrel and then the cold pale blossom of flame opening out against the brightness of her hair. This time the bullet took him squarely between the eyes; he hardly even felt it.

"VERY nice," said Johnny, "but not strictly necessary. The first would have been enough."

He transferred his attention for a moment to Valera's recumbent body; his face became thoughtful, withdrawn. "So he got Valera, did he? Some people are going to be cross about that."

"He wanted some action, didn't he?"

"Well, action was what he got. And rather more than he'd bargained for, by the look of things." Johnny moved absently forward, stopped as the pistol in Elsa's hand swung round to come into line with his navel. "Well, what happens now?"

"What happens now is that you keep still. I'm getting out of here."

"Going just where?"

"Never mind. Take your gun out and drop it on the floor. Move slowly."

Johnny sighed. "I haven't got a gun," he said. He knelt down, began to prise the pistol loose from Valera's clenched fingers. "Before we do anything else, we'd better make sure that the war's over, don't you think? Come on."

He went out and down the corridor. Elsa hesitated for a moment, then followed him. They paused inside the guardroom, staring at the desolation of smashed furniture, at the two twisted corpses; then Fedora moved quickly to the front door, peered cautiously out from behind the lintel. He came back dangling the pistol by the trigger-guard, his shoulders sagging slightly. "It looks as though it's all over," he said. "Just about a clean sweep. I must say I hadn't expected anything quite so thorough."

"How many of them?"

"There's two out there. Both dead. That's what you'd suppose—two to create the diversion, one to do the job. The classic method, in fact. Nearly came off. I wouldn't have wanted it any closer." He took her by the arm, led her through to the room where he and Valera once, a long time ago, had conversed. Even there, plaster had fallen from the ceiling and the smell of cordite hung in the air. "He was pretty fast with that knife of his. I really thought I'd had it. Lucky you pressed the button when you did."

She sat down in the armchair that still bore the imprint of Valera's bulky body and began to tremble. Fedora took down the bottle of Soberano from the sideboard, began to fill two glasses; looking, as he did so, out of the window. The hills and the rocks were there, grey in the starlight; the silence seemed so deep now as to have an actual weight, to be physically tangible. Invisible to the south was the sea, somewhere in the distance beyond the darkness; out there the *Polarlys* would be moving, and Moreno aboard her. "Here you are," he said, handing her one of the glasses. "Nothing to worry about. Just reaction. I've got a touch of the jitters myself, if it comes to that. That's why I'm talking too much."

She drank the cognac, put the glass down on the table. Fedora sat down opposite her. "Had you ever seen him before?"

"Who?"

"Chummy."

"No. No, never."

"It was you he was after."

"I know."

". . . Scared?"

She shrugged. "In a way. It gives one a . . . a goat-and-a-tiger sort of feeling."

"Not much of a tiger, really," said Johnny. "At least, I expect they were the top of the tree in their own line, but it wasn't much of a tree to start with. Tough boys from Africa, that'd be my guess."

"I still have to get back," she said.

"Get back where?"

"To the yacht."

"The yacht's already sailed. Early this evening."

He watched her digesting this new information in apparent calm; she didn't seem to be particularly surprised. "I see. They *have* left me high and dry."

"Yes. Thrown to the wolves. It's an old Russian custom."

"But I'm still alive."

"By a fluke."

"I want to stay that way," she said with sudden passion. "I *like* being alive. I don't want to die. Not now. Not ever."

Fedora finished his cognac; he, too, put down his glass on the table, let his hand rest there, tremorless, immobile. "When did it happen?" he asked. A muscle jumped high up in his cheek.

"What?"

"Well. . . . This. To us."

She lifted her head to stare at him; and whatever it was she had intended to say changed into a peculiar noise halfway between a growl and a sigh. Fedora felt the vibration of it pulsing against his mouth as it pressed into the softness of her throat; while under his tensed hand a pulse hammered quietly, a steady rhythmic beat under her warm skin, urgent on the ball of his thumb. His eyes were closed, yet he was aware of colour, of a dark and flowing redness enveloping him; he could feel it, a dull flesh-textured crimson, the warm colour of blood and of Elsa's lips. *I can touch it*, he thought, out of the depths of his tiredness; *touching things, that's how we know they're real. Sexual pleasure and physical pain, the vast lost kingdoms of the body; touching things, that's how we know we're alive. Elsa's real; Elsa is alive. That other girl, the girl in the pool, that other warm infinity of slippery redness, that's nothing but a nightmare. That's Moreno's kind of reality. This is mine.*

". . . In the stars, I suppose," she said.

"What?"

"Romeo and Juliet. You know. Starcrossed lovers."

Johnny withdrew a little, looked down at her surprisedly. She sat very still in the armchair; her eyes were still closed, the shadows of the lashes long on her cheeks. "What are you talking about?"

"*No sé. Tienes razon. ?Qué vamos a hacer?*"

"*?Que quieres que hagamos?*"

"*La cosa logica es hacer el amor.*"

"*Caramba. ?Ahora?*"

"*Si, ahora. Y despues descansaremos. ?Te parece?*" He felt the touch of her hand at the nape of his neck. "*Anda. Llevame en brazos.*"

"You're crazy as a coot," said Fedora.

He slipped an arm under her thighs and lifted her from the chair. She was heavier than he had expected, but far from unmanageable. He carried her through to the side room, where his travelling-case stood in the corner at the foot of the camp bed; it was almost dark there, but the curtains had not as yet been drawn and starlight filtered palely through the window. He pushed the door to with his foot and held her close against him, his hands tangled in the vague black cloud of her hair; her tongue felt taut and hard inside his mouth, her nails dug fiercely into the skin beneath his shoulder-blades. This kiss was as real as the other had been, but far more immediate. His hands, moving down her body, touched her arms; his own shoulders seemed to jerk in protest. "Damn," he said. "Sorry."

"It's all right."

"We'd better do something about it, all the same."

He went back through the guardroom; walked over to the rack where the Civil Guards' emergency packs were stored. He opened one and, after a few moments' rummaging, unearthed a regulation First Aid box; then went back to the bedroom, switched on the light. Elsa lay now on the bed, face downwards, the bathrobe on the floor beside her and her hair spread out over the pillow. Fedora sat down, took a tube of petroleum jelly from the tin and began to doctor the red burn-rashes on her arms, her shoulders, her feet. He worked slowly and carefully, coaxing an unusual gentleness into his strong brown pianist's fingers. "Your feet ought to be bandaged," he said in the end. "I haven't got one."

Elsa turned over, resting her weight on her left elbow. "I don't want one. It isn't necessary."

"I could tear up a shirt."

"All right." Her hand reached up to his collar, jerked it open. "Tear up *this* one."

Fedora sighed. "You've got a one-track mind," he said.

He crossed the room once more to turn off the light. He undressed by the window, feeling the cool night air of the sierra on his arms and chest; it was a long time since the simple awareness of being alive had given him so complete and undiluted a pleasure. And Elsa, after all, was right; this was the only possible way to celebrate. He took Valera's pistol from his pocket and laid it on the table beside the empty glasses, and he thought for a moment of Valera as he walked towards the bed. Pleasure and pain, pain and pleasure; like a medal with two sides and an indecipherable inscription. It didn't make sense, none of it. Reason had no part to play at all. Valera was dead and they were alive, and the two facts were quite unconnected. And so there wasn't a problem. No problem at all.

Elsa lay stretched out on the turned-back sheets, relaxed, abandoned as though to the sea or to death itself; like a drowned body, Ophelia or Leander, lost in voluptuousness. He knelt down beside her, and under the hardness of his mouth her body became alive, hot, hungry, passionate; he heard the breath rasping in her throat, the same intense, half-animal sound he had heard before, and her hands reached up for him, drew him towards her. And the redness slowly turned to a throbbing blackness full of movement, a curtain that swayed with the surging of the dark tides deep within their bodies, irresistible yet impersonal as the force that brings alien planets into unwilling orbit. Outside, a night of stars. The insects that had been startled into silence were now back in force, and the courtyard was urgent with the soft broken chirping of the crickets. A night of small rustlings and of searchings. She sobbed, in an ecstasy of anguish, against his shoulder; and he held her close.

IT took Fedora less than half-an-hour to go through Valera's papers and the report that his secretary had left three-quarters typed; they were not especially revealing—Valera, after all, had not been a man to omit obvious precautions—but they gave Fedora adequate food for thought. He sat for another hour at the old deal table with the table-lamp angled over the thin cardboard folders, not reading but thinking, smoking Valera's cigarettes; a little before midnight, he got up and went back to his room. Elsa was asleep; but she woke as he lay down beside her and turned over, feeling for his face with her right hand. "Where've you been?"

"Looking at Valera's papers."

"What's the time?"

"Just gone midnight." He bit gently at the back of her thumb. "It's a bad habit, you know."

"What is?"

"To wake up asking questions."

"I expect you're right. What did you want to see Valera's papers for?"

"To find out exactly what he was doing."

"You mean you didn't trust him?"

"It never got as far as that. You don't think he *told* me about it?"

"Didn't he?"

"Of course not."

"Then what have you got to *do* with it, exactly?"

"I told you."

"Yes, but officially? Are you Anglo-Spanish liaison, or what?"

"Nothing of the kind. He arrested *me*, as well."

"What for?"

"He didn't believe it, either."

"Believe what?"

"That I'm only in this thing by accident."

"And are you?"

"That's how it is."

Elsa groaned faintly. "These surrealistic conversations one gets into round about midnight. I suppose it all makes some kind of sense, but I'm damned if I know what it is."

"Yes," said Johnny. "Sorry. Must be the effects of Valera's prose style, which is kind of gnomic, if you know what I mean."

"I do. Others mightn't. Did *anything* emerge?"

"Oh yes. One thing's quite clear. Moreno worked for the Russians in the last war as a double agent, handing on information he got from the Spaniards. And as his job in Spain was U-boat maintenance and supply, a lot of the information he got was very useful. Useful to us, though—the English—not to the Russians. So the Russians lent him to us for a spell. We were on the same side, then. Funny."

"The Russians and the English were. The Spaniards weren't."

"They were neutral."

"Neutral, yes. They just supplied and serviced U-boats. That was all."

"And Moreno told us just where their assignation

points were, so that an R.A.F. Sunderland could sort of happen by and drop a bomb on them. It worked out about even."

Elsa's hand moved down to his shoulder, settled there as gently as a moth. He envied her delicacy of touch. "And you still don't know what it was he wanted from the swimming-pool?"

"I could make a good guess," said Johnny. "The records of the sinkings. Their exact locations. The supply team's logbooks, in fact. Logbooks are one of the few things that don't spoil under water."

". . . Give me a cigarette," said Elsa.

Johnny took cigarettes from the packet he had left on the table, struck a match. He watched her as she leaned forward to take the flame, her face rigid in the sharp red light, her drawn-up thighs emerging round and smooth from the dark shadows. "It was the last one of all," she said. "It was sunk a few days before the war ended, and Hellman was on it. We only found that out six months ago."

Johnny lit his own cigarette, shook out the match. "Who was Hellman?"

"He was the head of Moreno's organisation. Chief of Nazi liaison in Madrid. Do you know who is the head of the Spanish secret police?"

"No," said Johnny, and smiled.

"Nor do we. But Hellman did." The cigarette glowed abruptly against her mouth, held in her loosely-clenched fingers. "He helped to organise it. He laid down the plans, he brought in all the people who're now the top men, the heads of departments. And when that boat was sunk, he was running off to Argentina to form a private Gestapo for Peron—on Spanish lines. He had all the details of the Spanish C.E. systems with him—in a waterproof safe. They'll still be there." The cigarette-end stabbed downwards. ". . . A long way under."

"But good God," said Fedora. "Is that all?"

"How do you mean?"

"That was fifteen years ago, for God's sake."

"Nothing's changed. Franco's still in, and things don't change much in Spain anyway. Besides—when you have something good, you hang on to it."

"You think the Spanish secret police are *good*?"

"Better than ours, maybe. Don't *you* think so?"

"It all depends," said Johnny cautiously, "on what you happen to want a secret police force for."

"All I know is that Head Office thinks those papers are important. We still have high hopes for Spain, you know; all the factors that caused the Civil War are still floating around . . . in suspended animation, you might say. . . . When Franco goes, that's when the balloon'll be sent up. If we knew just how to paralyse his police system and if we could get in first with our *putsch*, then the balance of things would swing our way. I don't have to tell you that. You know it's true."

"It's been known to happen that way before, of course," Johnny admitted. He was staring sightlessly now at the dark ceiling, his head beside Elsa's on the hard pillow. "It'd be a slap in the eye for the Americans if you *did* pull it off. Yes, I can see it'd be worth a gamble."

"It's a highly centralised system—that much we *do* know. It all rotates round one man in just the same way as the Cabinet revolves round Franco. The top man is the man who counts. *He*'s the one that Fer. . . . that all our people are after."

They smoked in silence for a while. In the end, Johnny leaned sideways to stub out his cigarette on the floor and said,

"Whoever it is must want those papers too."

"Obviously. They're dangerous. But why do you say that?"

"Because Valera must have been playing the old cat-and-mouse game. They let Moreno escape in the first place; and then, even when they must have guessed Moreno was on the yacht, they didn't try to arrest him. They arrested *you* instead, hoping to force your people into moving too quickly. They want Moreno to lead them to the papers, don't you see?—that's what they've wanted all along. Valera must have thought I was playing exactly the same game on behalf of British Intelligence. It all fits together all right, in a lunatic sort of a way."

"But you said the *Polarlys* had sailed already?"

"So it has. They couldn't take a chance on you not talking—that's how Valera was twisting their arms. But then he didn't expect *this* kind of a counter." Johnny waved his arm vaguely in the darkness towards the guardroom and the corridor. "It's like you said—in the secret police, things tend to revolve round one man. Now Valera's dead, it may be a little while before they can pull all the threads together again. That's what they're planning on—Moreno and your other pal whose name begins with F. They won't be wasting any time. Listen," he said, and turned his head sideways on the pillow. "Do you know where they're going?"

"I was there when they marked up the chart, yes. I've got a rough idea."

"How far is it?"

"About four hours."

"*Four hours?* They'll be there already, then."

"I don't suppose they'll have gone straight there. They couldn't dive until it's light enough to see. And they can't rely on finding the wreck straight off. Even when you have an accurate fix, these things take some looking for."

"He's a good navigator, is he?"

"Very good. His name is Feramontov."

"*Feramontov?*" said Johnny; and there was a long silence. ". . . . Yes," he said in the end. "I've heard of *him*."

"Yes. And he's heard of *you*."

In the next room, the telephone screamed shrilly. Johnny felt Elsa's body stiffen into rigidity at his side; they lay still for a moment, listening to the long high-pitched peals of the buzzer coming through the darkness. Then Fedora sat up.

"I'd better answer it . . . I suppose. . . . "

DEEP under the Rock of Gibraltar, neon lights burn perpetually. They illuminate twenty-one miles of tunnels; wide roads down which lorries and ammunition trucks rumble with a noise like that of a distant explosion of dynamite, narrow concrete-lined passages down which men in military uniform move silently, on crepe-rubber heels, carrying sheaves of typewritten papers or leather despatch-cases with gold-embossed crests. There are doors that slide open at a touch and there are doors that are kept locked and have no keyhole; at each turning are gaily-painted signs that bear bewildering sequences of initials and numbers, GPRO 71 and DOCinC, HQMVODI and CE 7, all beneath the broad bands of colour that form the only signposts in the nearest thing to a rabbit-warren that human ingenuity can yet have devised. Trout sat on a very comfortable chair directly beneath the neon light in a hutch of a room filled with filing cabinets; a room known to the General Indexing System as NI 12 Double Red—the Archives Section of Naval Intelligence, Gibraltar—and more briefly, to the inhabitants of the neighbouring hutches, as the Pardonable Error Shop. The native genius of the place, Commander Macfarlane, R.N., sat behind a high barricade of filing trays and mumbled, ostensibly to Trout but really to himself. His unintelligibility was largely due to the meerschaum pipe clenched in his excellent teeth: Vice-Admiral Crane was known to hold that pipe-smokers were solid men, and Macfarlane had a reputation for brilliance to live down. Eventually, and as Trout had known he would do, he removed the object, glanced at it with some distaste, and said,

"Well, it looks like Feramontov."

"Wonderful," said Trout, who was feeling somewhat tired. "Amazing, Holmes."

Macfarlane placed the pipe down on the desk, where it instantly went out. "Ever heard of him?"

"It rings a bell."

"So it ought to. He's one of the few people that the Russkies always seem to have around whenever they have a project afoot that . . . well, whenever the sky's the limit. Not a very good metaphor, in view of the Sputniks. But that's a case in point. When the Russians go for something, they throw in everything but the kitchen sink."

"And send for Feramontov, the Bulbul Emir."

"That's about it. I'll give you the most recent items on the record, to show you what I mean. 1946 to 1951 . . . in the United States, working in the A-bomb spy-ring. 1952 . . . Persia and Afghanistan, pepping up the Mussadeq mob. '53 to '55, in East Berlin. In '56 he was in Egypt and in '57 he was in Hungary. Since then he's been reported in Moscow, in Berlin again, in China and last year in North Africa—Red Hand stuff in Algeria, more precisely. What you might call a bit of a trouble-shooter."

"Well, and now he's in Spain. Which seems to be the point. If it *is* him, just what does he want with Moreno?"

"What does he want with the *Polarlys?* is really more

the question. Deep-sea diving, that isn't his usual line. I must say your theory seems to make some sense, as far as it goes, but if it's one of Moreno's U-boats he's after . . . one asks oneself, what for?"

"Quite so. And does one get an answer?"

"No. One doesn't. We can probably get the positions all right—Archie Lane's running through the archives now—but once we've got them, I don't quite see what we can do about it."

"You could patrol them, couldn't you?" said Trout, and yawned profoundly. "Until the *Polarlys* shows up. Then you'll know which is the right one. And can act accordingly."

Macfarlane picked up his pipe again and gnawed at the end of it for a while. "We could send a corvette, all right. Not that I suppose old Reynolds'd be all that keen on shooting her off at a moment's notice without a rather better excuse than the one we've got. As for the act-accordingly part . . . that's not so easy, either. We can't very well go in for this diving racket ourselves, and if—as is quite likely—the wreck's in Spanish territorial waters, we won't be able even to *approach* it. And there's nothing they can do about the *Polarlys*, either, assuming they have sense enough to keep moving. We can't board her at speed and we can't shoot her up, that'd be piracy on the high seas. I mean, there's some things you can't expect even the Navy to do."

"Well, and what about Johnny?"

"Fedora? Well, we'll take legal advice on that point," said Macfarlane cheerfully. "No doubt we can make some kind of representation to the Spanish authorities, though you'll realise it can't very well be done through *us*. Between you and me, I very much doubt if there's an awful lot that you can do."

"That's what I thought," said Trout glumly. "In fact, he's had his chips. The poor old sausage."

". . . Valera?" said the telephone, in a raspy voice. Fedora moved the receiver a little farther away from his ear.

"No. The Captain's asleep. He asked not to be disturbed, except in case of emergency."

"Yes, well, who's speaking? Cremades?"

"Yes, this is Cremades."

"Right. Lopez here. Speaking from Malaga. I've got the report here, you want me to dictate it?"

"Go ahead."

"*Polarlys* last picked up by radar at 2340 hours, still headed south-east. Position then some twenty-two kilometres south-south-west of Fuengirola. Helicopter pilot reports visibility excellent, but there may be some sea mist rising in the early morning, thinning out to heat haze. There's a message from Madrid reminding the captain to file his report before noon tomorrow, you want me to give it to you word for word?"

"No, that's all right. I'll remind him."

"Good. Report ends there. What are the instructions? Are we to go on checking the ship, or what?"

"No," said Fedora. "That's no longer necessary."

A pause.

"The pilots are to stand off, then?"

"That's for *you* to say. Valera says to call the hunt off, that's all I know. He probably knows where they're heading for, anyway."

"The girl's talked, has she?"

"*I* don't know. But I don't suppose the Captain would be sleeping, if she hadn't."

"*Hombre, !estupendo! Enhorabuena.* You'll be calling us later, then."

"Yes. Later."

"*Bueno, Cremades. Muy buenas noches.*"

"*Lo mismo digo,*" said Fedora, and hung up. The palms of his hands were sweating lightly. He went back to the bedroom; "Elsa," he said. "Hey, Elsa. . . . "

Elsa didn't move. She was asleep.

THE coffin scraped into its niche in the high white wall. The bearers stepped back, crossing themselves a little nervously, and the plasterer came forward; began to slap the wet cement into place, to build up the thin double *tabique* that would wall the coffin off from the world of the living. The mourners watched in silence. When the plasterer had finished his task to his own satisfaction, he took a hammer and drove a hook into the wall above the niche; reached up to hang upon it two small wreaths of Marbella roses. Another man, dressed in black, stepped forward and traced initials with his finger in the wet plaster; C.F.S. for Carmen Figueroas Sanchez. Slowly, the watchers began to turn away. The funeral was over.

There was time to walk back to the village before the sun rose high enough to become oppressive. The cheap funerals were always early. Only the fashionable ones took place in the evening. Fedora, who had meant to pay for a first-class funeral and hadn't had time to make the offer, felt a little guilty about this. He wasn't even wearing a black suit. He hadn't been at all surprised that people had looked at him and whispered. He thought it very natural. He might, after all, have been the one that had done it. He was a stranger; that made him an obvious suspect. People stepped aside from him as he walked down the path between the high white walls studded with memorial plaques, under the

Moorish arch with its wrought-iron gate.

From the road outside the cemetery, he could see the village spread out to his right; church tower, cypress spire, fronds of palm; and behind the village, the sea. And on the sea, a pale white ship leaving a hairline of foam. It wasn't the *Polarlys*, of course; but it might have been. It served as a reminder.

Fedora leaned his back against the cemetery wall and lit a cigarette. Half past nine; already it was hot; here on the high ground the sea breezes scarcely had strength left to be felt against the cheek. The villagers walked past him, coming out through the iron gates in twos and threes; some of them looked at him curiously again, but others didn't look at him at all. Eventually, three young men went by; two of them were talking animatedly to each other, while the third had his eyes on the ground and said nothing at all. Fedora threw his cigarette away and fell into step beside them. "Garcia," he said. "Could I speak to you for a moment?"

"*Sí, señor. Desde luego.*"

"You know who I am, I suppose?"

The young man nodded, still without having looked up.

"I want you to do something for me. You and your brothers. I need some help, and pretty urgently."

The young man walked on; the other two men were now also silent, silent and slightly hostile. Fedora didn't find their attitude at all encouraging; he wondered what to say next. "It wasn't me that did it, you know," he said. "Maybe some people say so. Some people will say anything. And if you think I should have prevented it happening, well, perhaps I should. But they're not much use, are they?—all these should-haves and might-have-beens. All I want to do now is find the man who killed her. That's all. And like I say, you can help me. That's if you want to."

Black toecaps, scuffling in the dust. ". . . Some people think *I* did it," said Garcia. "The Civiles—*they* thought so, at first. Had me up before the Señor Juez. I didn't do it, though, of course I didn't. I wouldn't do a thing like that, *Dios lo sabe*."

An oddly deep voice with a thick *malagueño* accent, blurred consonants and sibilants strangled at birth. And a muscle that twitched at the side of his mouth as he spoke. And eyes, liquid and deep and brown, turning at last in Johnny's direction. "Just what did you want me to do to help?" he said.

AN hour later that morning, Fedora walked down past the brightly-painted bungalows with their scraps of withered garden to the steps that led down to the beach; and from the steps he walked past the wooden beach-huts and the noisy open-air bars and the sprawled-out groups of sunbathing Spaniards towards the lighthouse. He walked through a world of cheerful, extrovert holidaymakers, and as he walked he felt again that sense of isolation, of being as far removed from all hope of genuine communication as a visitor from another planet or a dog. On the beach were well over a thousand people, come to Marbella from all parts of Spain and now engaged in doing nothing and in thinking nothing, in spending their vacations as vacantly as they possibly could; Fedora picked his way amongst them, looking at them and at the sea as though both were obvious natural phenomena, most manifestly *there* but, in another way, not. The sunbathers and the mourners, the beach and the cemetery. . . . They formed a background, that was all, to such events as those of the previous night, events of which they knew nothing and in no way participated; Fedora and Valera, Elsa and Feramontov, with their plans and *putsches*, their schemes, attacks and assassinations, shared at least their difference from those other people, shared another kind of reality. There they all were—taking the sun, dipping their feet, drinking beer, thinking nothing, doing nothing, just *living*; Fedora watched them, and the awareness of his own loneliness moved all the time inside him like a kind of fear. He walked on, and eventually found Elsa stretched out on the sand in front of the lighthouse; she wore a tight yellow bathing suit with the shoulder straps unfastened, lay face down on a big towel with green and yellow stripes, and she seemed to be asleep. Then, as he sat down beside her, she lifted her head and opened her eyes. "You're late," she said.

"A little."

"I was afraid you might not come."

"I was afraid you mightn't be here."

"I was feeling lonely."

"I know," said Johnny. "So was I."

He lay back on the edge of the towel, and the weight of the sun pressed redly against his eyelids. Elsa looked at him and, after a moment, reached out to rub her forefinger along the line of his collarbone inside his shirt, from neck to shoulder curve and back again. Her touch was like a sculptor's, Fedora thought, working in clay; a caress to her was a means of self-expression. "You bought the stuff?" he asked.

"Yes. All we need. I had to spend all the money you gave me, though."

"Never mind," said Fedora lazily. "We won't need money where we're going."

"That *does* sound despondent."

"I didn't mean it that way."

"And Garcia?"

"Yes. He'll take us."

"When?"

"Now," said Johnny.

He sat up abruptly. Their bare arms touched, a

physical contact as sudden and intimate as an electric shock; Elsa's lips came half-open. They weren't looking at each other and didn't try to do so; it wasn't necessary. They were looking down the beach towards the mole; where, one by one, the fishing boats were running out from the warm sands to ride on the breeze-ruffled water. Brown singleted figures set the sails and the boats moved away in slow procession, dancing gently as they passed the mole and the current took possession of their hulls; then other brown figures came splay-footed over the sands, heaving another boat down to the water's edge and splashing heavily through the foam to pull themselves aboard. The morning sun beat smoothly down, striking reflection from the sea's blue surface; all the world was of colour and of shivering fragments of light, was the scent of the sea and the grittiness of the sand and the salt muscular warmth of Elsa's skin; and Johnny watched it all for a few moments and then sighed and got to his feet. While Elsa, herself briefly a part of it, sat curled up on the towel, her eyes wide open under the shelter of her hand.

"I don't ever want to die," she said again.

Fedora looked down at her and smiled. "I know," he said. "You're tired of being lonely. It's a hard life for a pretty girl . . . always was."

"And you? Don't *you* get tired?"

"Sometimes, yes. Tired and afraid. But I'm that way by nature. That's why I can't do more than . . . help a little. But remember me, won't you?—when you're one of *them*."

"It was fun being helped," said Elsa. "I wouldn't want to forget."

She, too, stood up; and Johnny reached down to pick

up the heavy canvas bag that lay behind her, hoisting it
with an effort across his shoulders. "It's all here?"

"Yes."

"And you haven't changed your mind?"

"No."

"All right," said Johnny. "Come on, then."

MORENO wasn't his real name, of course. His real
name had long since been forgotten, though it
must have been Spanish because his father had
been Spanish—a minor administrative official in
Tetuan. He had died of typhus, though, when Moreno
was four years old, and his Moorish wife—who had
then been just nineteen—had taken the child and a
small bundle of personal possessions to Tangier; where
she had begun to earn her living in a long and draughty
house full of closed doors and swinging bead curtains,
where lizards moved jerkily over the white walls. He
remembered the first-floor room with the truckle bed
and its dry, slightly rancid smell; that was where his
long sad odyssey had really begun, a journey like an
endless pilgrimage to many cities and to many countries;
and from that time, perhaps, could be dated his hatred
of women and his vast contempt for men. Now Moreno
was his name, and that was enough.

He stood on deck now with his great arms resting on
the guardrail, and from behind his thoughtless brown
pupils he looked out at the coast of Spain in the morning; the long, sprawled-out coast that the yacht was
dragging along behind it, the great grey sweep of the
bay, the colourless sand and the faded jagged wood-
smoke blue of the mountains. And for once he *was*
thinking of the past; trying to remember just how it
had been before and failing to do so, just as he usually

failed when he tried to summon the past to his aid.

Before, of course, it had been dark, or almost dark, an almost moonless night though the whole sky had been prickly with stars, and what he best remembered—almost the only thing—was the roar of engines overhead, the sudden presence of wide wings crowding out the stars and passing swiftly on, the pencil-beam of sparkling light converging on a grey and glistening hull, and then the violent orange corona of leaping flame blistering abruptly upwards from the tortured sea. Explosion: violence: murder. The images echoed in the depths of his vague mind like the twangs of a radar set, reverberating like distant gongs. Violence: murder: death. . . .

And his thoughts went twisting away like a shoal of little fishes, picking up as they fled the last flash of life in deep surprised brown eyes at the water's surface; white legs scattering the bubbles; white hands clutching for the air as his own hands, dark and powerful and quite remorseless, guided in the chisel. Moreno's lower lip fell open, his tongue slithered loosely over it; his face, with the bright light of morning glancing off the high Arab cheekbones, became as though haunted. Feramontov, coming up at that moment to stand at the guardrail beside him, saw his expression and waited a tactful few seconds before speaking.

". . . Remember anything, Moreno?"

Moreno smiled; Feramontov wondered why. Then, after a pause,

"It was different, you see. It was dark. One bit of sea is much like another."

Feramontov nodded. "Well, we're almost there," he said. "You and Meuvret had better get ready."

He lowered his head to light a cigarette, shielding the flame with his hand. "We'll dive as soon as we possibly can," he said, looking up again. "There's no time to waste."

"A pity, in some ways," said Moreno smoothly, "about Elsa."

"You two will manage. Meuvret's done plenty of diving and he has experience of these waters. You'll have to watch out for the undertow."

"I suppose there's no news?"

"News?"

"Of Elsa?"

"We're not expecting any," said Feramontov. "We had best conveniently forget that the lady ever existed."

He watched Moreno walk away over the well-scrubbed deckboards; straight back, immense shoulders, high-held arrogant head. Physical beauty, the most perishable of assets in a man or a woman; a pity, he thought, that it should ever have to be destroyed before its time. Yes, it had been a pity about Elsa. Yet no one could be trusted . . . no one at all. . . .

Perhaps, in the last resort, not even himself. . . .

THE sea, faintly marbled with foam, slapped and gurgled against the hull of the fishing-boat; it was calm, though, the waves no more than topped by a slow breeze from Africa. The *Polarlys*, half a mile away and drawing steadily nearer, seemed etched against the blue of the horizon, motionless as though painted there. "They're stopped, all right," said Garcia, easing the tiller over a fraction. "On a sea anchor, I should think."

"Aim to pass her to the north. Not nearer than half a kilometre."

"Right you are."

Fedora stared for a few moments more at the distant yacht, then moved forward to where Elsa sat with the canvas bag between her slim brown knees. "It looks like this is it. What do you think?"

"I'd say so, yes. But I'm no navigator."

"You're a swimmer."

"Oh, *that*. Well, it could be worse. There'll be a hell of an undercurrent, but it's in our favour . . . as far as *getting* there's concerned."

Fedora sat down beside her. "Will *they* have gone down yet?"

"They wouldn't wait around."

"Moreno and . . . ?"

"Probably Meuvret."

"Not Feramontov?"

"No."

"They'll miss *you*, won't they?"

"Probably. Three pairs of flippers are better than two. But they'll manage."

"We'd better get ready."

"Yes."

She opened the bag, began to take out the skin-diving equipment. Fedora took off his shirt and trousers; then they dressed each other in silence. Weighted belt, with sheath-knife and torch; the flippers; the mask; lastly, the canvas carrier with the compressed-air cylinders. Fedora wondered, as he slid the harness over Elsa's naked shoulders, how it would chafe against the freshly-formed blisters, how the salt water would knife at her burns. Pain, he thought; always pain; he was sick of pain. "It's going to be cold, you know," said Elsa, "without a suit."

"I thought you said you didn't wear them."

"Nor we do, usually. But we may have to go down rather deep this time. Still, there it is." Her fingers moved over the valve control, checking the pressure. "Set yours at five, to start with. The regulator. Right?"

"Right," said Fedora, testing.

"I don't like suits, anyway. So hard to get all the air out of them before you begin." She pushed the mask up over her forehead, smoothed the lastex of her swimsuit down past her hips; signs of nervousness, thought Fedora. He could hardly blame her. He leaned forward and ran his lips along the line of her cheek, touching with the tip of his tongue the warm salty skin. "It's all right," she said. "I'll get you there."

"You're just afraid it may be a one-way trip."

"I wish it wasn't Moreno down there. That's all."

"If it wasn't Moreno," said Johnny, "I doubt if I'd

feel much like going."

He watched her thinking about Moreno. Her dislike of him, of course, was mostly instinctive: as was her dislike of certain flat-headed, bulbous fish that it cost her an effort to touch. She *did* touch them, though; she dissected them; she drew little diagrams of their inner organs. Now she leaned over the bulwarks of the little boat beside Fedora, her elbow within an inch of his, and stared down into the swirling depths beneath her. "I'll bet," she said, "that no one's remembered to feed my jellyfish."

"Never mind. There's as good jellyfish in the sea as ever came out of it."

"I still think it's a shame."

Rope-soled feet scraped on the coaming above them. One of the Garcia brothers looked down at them, nodded briefly, then turned away. "Well," said Fedora. "Here we go."

He touched her arm lightly; then seated himself on the gunwale, toppled himself quickly over backwards and sank like a stone.

A T five fathoms' depth a dimness enveloped him, a gloom like a blue-green twilight, though he was aware as he swam of a vast refulgence high above him, the tremor of the sunlight on the waves. Elsa he could see as a dark shape swimming below him and slightly to his left, could trace by the chains of bubbles rising from her mask. Now and again he sensed, rather than saw, a fleeting whiteness beneath him as they passed over patches of smooth sand.

As the minutes moved by, he saw more clearly; the light seemed to filter down through the water, and with it came a semblance of colour. The sands below took on a yellowish tinge, broken by wide green-brown bars of rock; but there was nothing to serve as a landmark, other than the ceaseless pull of the undertow. Here they were on the edge of the Gibraltar Straits, where the great vacuum of the Mediterranean draws millions of gallons daily from the open Atlantic; Elsa had warned him of the strength of that current, but he had never quite realised the vastness of its power. He was relying on that current to carry him eventually to the shore, some four miles distant; Fedora was a fairly good swimmer, but he had never swum so great a distance in his life, and was well aware that—even with the help of flippers, aqualung, and current, even with Elsa's guidance—the risk he was taking was considerable. The air in the cylinders would probably give out before he reached the land; and the surface currents, unlike those of the depths, were unpredictable.

But Elsa swam on unhesitantly, and Johnny followed her. Far to the right a shoal of fish pivoted and moved away, their bodies gleaming dully as they turned like the fuselages of banking aeroplanes; then they disappeared into a sudden shimmer of vague colour, the fringes of a huge seaweed forest. Long bare shoulders of rock came wriggling now towards him, building out of nowhere a pattern of grey and black shadows; the scenery was changing. He wondered for how long a time they had been swimming, and looked at his wrist-watch. Twelve minutes. It seemed rather longer.

Then he saw Elsa signal with her hand, and he rolled half over in order to look upwards. A long fishlike shape, outlined in winking diamonds of water; this time he knew at once what it was. The *Polarlys*, forty feet above them. He realised that Elsa was beginning to circle, though he had no real sense of any change of direction; not until, three minutes or so later, they turned full into the current and it was like trying to swim against a moving and invisible wall. But it was at that moment that the first faint vibrations came to them through the water—the feel, rather than the sound, of a slow, rhythmic *tongggggk*, *tongggggk*, *tongggggk*. He saw Elsa's sunbrown body turning against the undertow, her hands outstretched now as though in search of that vast, dim throbbing; then she dived and again he followed her, sinking fast with the sweep of the current towards the ocean floor.

The tall rocks rose around them. The darkness increased noticeably, and so did the pressure against his eardrums. Then he saw the light. Not the splintered

fragments of light he had grown used to, sparks reflected
downwards by the waves far above him, but a bright,
steady, focused beam, such as he might have seen on
land. It seemed to move, to grow and then to diminish
in intensity as they swam towards it; it was lower even
than they were, at the sea's very bottom. Another light
suddenly shone full on him, took him in the eyes with a
terrible intensity, then turned away; he saw, as it
turned, the sea bed, white sand and black rock, a
phantasmagoria of twisted shadows some fifteen feet
below him. He hadn't been seen, he told himself: here,
he was just one moving shade amongst a thousand
others. Only the leaping bubbles might give him
away. . . .

Down now amongst the rocks, huge shapes crawling
about him; invisible yet threatening presences, like
ghosts of extinct monsters; sixty feet beneath the surface,
at least, in the lost dim world of Atlantis. Davy Jones'
locker, thought Fedora, sculling himself on from rock to
rock; dark, cold and dismal; the floor of the Mediterranean, powdered with the dust of sailors' bones; the
skeletons of Phoenician merchants, of Moorish corsairs,
of German submariners and of English sailors, all
ground to powder by the underwater tides. That light
again, directly in front of him now; first one torch, then
the other; and suddenly he saw the great long grey
whalebacked sandscoured sunken shape, enormous in
the pencil-beams, hulking broken-spined on the tortur-
ing rocks; and he sank noiselessly to shelter among the
seaweed fronds, clutching at their shiny straps with his
hands to hold himself in place against the constant,
wearying pull of the current. The U-boat lay before
him, its battered conning-tower not twenty feet away

and its long streamlined hull stretching away illimitably
to either side. Two figures moved in the water, hovering
just above the conning-tower, and the torches spread
their pallid stains of light over the dull metal as the
figures circled. The hammering had now stopped. The
hatch had been forced open. Nosing downwards like
browsing fish, the hovering figures disappeared, one by
one, inside.

FULL marks, then, to Feramontov for his navigation. And, of course, to Elsa. She had found the U-boat; had arrived, moreover, very opportunely. Fedora found himself wondering exactly what to do, now that he'd got there. Of course, he told himself savagely, he hadn't come all that way just to *watch*. On the other hand, he couldn't pretend that he much fancied his chances if it came to an underwater tangle with Moreno; clearly, it would be sensible to weigh the odds in his own direction as much as he possibly could. To use, in fact, surprise as a weapon. He turned his head, peered sideways through the mica of his visor. Elsa was there, a few feet to his left, wrapped almost to invisibility in the writhing seaweed. He signalled to her with his hand and began to swim forward.

Go in after them? Or wait till they came out? That last way, he could take them one by one. Yes, but it was only Moreno he was really worried about. And within the confines of the U-boat hull, Moreno would have less chance to use his superior skill as a swimmer. They might even have to fight in darkness, which would neutralise at a stroke all Moreno's natural advantages. There was no doubt about it, really. Fedora flippered his way up to the conning-tower and entered the U-boat as the others had done, edging his way in head downwards, Elsa close behind him.

Inside, the darkness was almost complete. He felt his

way uncertainly down into what he knew must be the
control room; he could hear once again faint vibrations,
was aware of glints of reflected light, of nearby movements. The blackness oppressed him, closed in upon
him like the walls of a tomb; he risked a quick flash
from his own torch, and saw the periscope pillar jump
into reality directly before him, tall and shadowy,
crusted in sea-acorns yet slimy to the touch. He pulled
himself down beside it, felt for Elsa and pressed her
down close against him. Farther down the hull, the
lights flickered dimly, then grew stronger.

A sudden flicker of greenish-silver as a bucketful of
tiny fishes came fleeing past them. Elsa's hand on his
wrist, holding him tightly. Then a great stream of light
that seemed to pin them both to the periscope column,
a whirling vortex of shadows, the twin torches returning
fast down the companionway.

Fedora glanced up at the strings of shining bubbles
that rose from their hiding-place towards the conning-
tower, glistening in the hard white light. They would
see those bubbles, of course—they couldn't miss them—
but they couldn't be sure as to their cause. A pocket of
air, maybe, trapped for years within the U-boat and
released by their movements. . . . They would investi-
gate, surely, and that would be his chance; perhaps his
only chance, insofar as Moreno was concerned. Johnny
braced his flippered feet against the slippery floor,
seeking a firm purchase; his right hand drew the knife
from his weighted belt. When they rounded the column,
that would be the moment. . . .

A torch suddenly appeared before him, bright as a
sun, staring straight into his face, and instantly he
launched himself at it with all his force. He held the

knife gripped with both hands in front of him, and the shock of its impact ran through his arms and shoulders. A few brief seconds of confused and shadowy whirling in the floodlit water and then he was clear, his victim falling away from him in almost comically slow motion, arms thrashing spasmodically at nothing and a great streamer of blood swinging magically outwards from his riven chest. Johnny was momentarily horrified at the ghastly effect of the blow, at the nightmare-like silence in which his opponent was dying; but already he knew that his luck was out, that he had killed the wrong man. Moreno had been bringing up the rear.

Meuvret's torch, spinning slowly towards the deck, caught in its beam for a second the great brown body with its lifted head, flashed on the blank eyepiece of the diving mask; in that moment, Moreno dropped his own torch and the blade of his own knife came flowing smoothly out into his hand. He was swimming too fast to change direction or to swerve away, too fast to give Fedora time to turn, and the two men collided awkwardly in a sudden bewilderment of tangled limbs and jerking bubbles; were lifted apart by the swirling water and were instantly twisting, circling, paddling wildly round to face each other like wrestlers, the torchlight spilling redly off the waiting knife-blades.

Moreno's finned feet flailed in the water as he came in again, fast and at chest level; Johnny dived to his right and across the beam of the fallen torches, hoping to be lost for a second in the darkness as he turned. He wheeled and found Moreno almost on top of him, turning to jab viciously downwards at his thighs; he twisted inwards and felt Moreno's weight cannon into his shoulder; caught mutually off-balance, they swayed

apart and span to face each other once more. Again
Johnny was seized by a sense of complete unreality, the
sense that he was taking part in a scene belonging to the
animal world rather than the human—a dark pre-
historic battle fought beneath the waves by giant
predators to whom survival was a matter of strength
and cruelty, of skill and cunning. He glimpsed Elsa out
of the corner of his eye; she was crouched now in the
corner, keeping Moreno in the beam of her torch and
trying whenever possible to shine the light full in his
eyes; that was why Moreno had missed an opportunity
just then. It made the odds a little more even, and
Fedora was rapidly learning; he knew now better than
to strike out at Moreno with all his strength, since the
water resisted the blow and pushed him away from his
target even as his hand descended. Moreno was taking
care now not to turn his back towards Elsa; almost
certainly he had recognised them both by now. Yes, or
was it that he . . . ?

Fedora's legs kicked out in a sudden reflex as Moreno
torpedoed himself through the water, straightening out
his long dark dangerous body in a swift and unexpected
plunge far to Fedora's left. The move had taken Elsa by
surprise, too; she dived away in a fan of bubbles . . . not
fast enough. A huge brown hand closed vicelike over
her ankle, pulled her to a halt; the wide shoulders
seemed to poise themselves for a second, then jerked as
the knife came veering wickedly in towards her belly.
With the movement there came a sound like the slap
of a heavy glove against a table, and in the same instant
something took Fedora around the chest and sucked
him violently forward; the breath was whipped from
his lungs and light blazed in his eyes; he felt a sudden

and unbearable vertigo, such as a spider might feel when being sucked down the whirlpool of the waste-pipe. His legs struck against something hard and unyielding, his fingers stang from contact with what must have been Elsa's diving-mask; his ears rattled with a dull, obscene gurgling noise, then burst with a tremendous booming clang. A hand closed over his left shoulder. . . .

Then Moreno and nothing but Moreno, a gigantic ominous shape looming over him, the bright knife swinging down towards his stomach as slowly as in a dream. Then a heave, and the whole world lurching sideways, Moreno with it; Elsa somewhere underneath him, first pushing him away than brought up hard against him, the unexpected yet familiar smoothness of her legs, clammy cold, pressing on his ribs . . . then she was gone, and in her place a narrow steel girder driving hard against his chest, and Moreno and the knife coming in at him again, fast this time, very fast and smooth. And his knee came up to jar against the sweep of Moreno's forearm, deflecting the thrust, and his own right hand came round in a clean half-circle, confident and almost casual, sinking his knife deep into Moreno's throat, ramming the hilt up tight against the cold brown skin. He drew it out, and a cloud of blood misted the visor of his mask. That was it. It was over. Moreno was dead.

THE safe stood in the corner of the officers' cabin, buckled almost to unrecognisability. Neither Moreno nor Meuvret had been an explosives expert, thought Johnny grimly as he surveyed the wreckage by torchlight; they had detonated enough 808 to have blown a hole in the hull itself, and in so doing had certainly saved Elsa's life. Moreno's blade had broken the skin in a line along her lower ribs; and that was all.

Johnny lowered his head and shoulders to peer inside the twisted safe door, playing the torch beam from side to side. The safe was empty, except for a waterproof lead-lined despatch case stamped with the initials, O.L.H. He showed it to Elsa, who nodded. They had found what they had come for. It had cost already a dozen lives, perhaps many more; and almost their own. Fedora looked at it. It is difficult to laugh inside a diving mask; he shrugged his shoulders, instead.

BACK in the control room Moreno's body still drifted, one leg now raised in a weird high-jumper's straddle. Johnny passed it by, directing the torch-beam up the shaft of the conning-tower; he and Elsa had a long swim before them, a very long swim, and already he felt tired. The hatch of the tower, he noticed, had fallen; shaken, maybe, by the blast of the explosion. He swam slowly up to it, pushed against it. Nothing happened. He felt for the steel rungs of the ladder, braced his feet against them, tried again. Elsa's hands and masked head appeared in the torchlight close beside him, thrusting, testing, helping him to push. But to no effect. The hatch was jammed, jammed tight. Fedora stared at it, and his stomach seemed suddenly to turn over in a wave of panic so powerful that he had to suppress a desire to vomit.

He looked for a few moments longer at Elsa's long competent fingers with their blunt nails, still probing desperately for an interstice in the hermetic sealing of the hatch; a small blue fish was poking its nose at the metal, too, as though also anxious to seek a way out. Was there any other way out? Probably not. Almost certainly not. All the same, Moreno's body had drifted some short way in the last few minutes; *some* current, at least, had to be passing down the hull. Fedora pushed himself away from the ladder, descended in a slow spiral to the control room once again.

He found what he was hunting for halfway down the
companionway; a long, rectangular rent low down in
the submarine's grey steel skin; a good six feet long, but
nowhere more than nine or ten inches wide. This, he
thought, was clearly where the bomb had struck that
had finished off the U-boat. But the metal seemed to
have been in no way weakened by the explosion; the
edges of the fissure were razor-sharp in places, and he
cut his wrist while exploring one ragged lip. He withdrew; Elsa was close behind him, watching intently.
He shook his head and swam on.

During the next fifteen minutes they investigated the
rest of the hull. It was an unnerving experience. Most
of the ship's equipment and furnishings had survived
intact under a film of slime; on one of the bunks they
found a sailor's skeleton, hardly disturbed, and farther
down the ship a skull lay with complete incongruousness
on top of a plotting table, as though someone had
placed it there five minutes before. The little fishes that
had been frightened by the explosion were now back in
their dozens, except for a few who had been too close
and who now floated, belly upwards, overhead. Fedora
tried to trace the point where the fishes were entering,
but found nothing other than a hole the size of his fist
beside the torpedo-room bulkhead.

He had a sudden ridiculous longing to smoke a
cigarette. His mind was fast becoming a blank, was
failing to receive the most obvious of sensory impres-
sions. When he looked at his wrist-watch, he had to
concentrate on the dial to be sure of what it said. He
looked towards Elsa, jerked his thumb towards the air
cylinder on his back. She raised one hand with the
fingers outstretched; five minutes more. That made it a

grim lookout, thought Johnny.

They each carried only a single cylinder, because they hadn't had enough money to buy any more. Meuvret and Moreno had been working on double cylinders, and since Elsa had been prudent enough to close the valves it was reasonable to suppose there was a good deal of air left in them. The trouble was that, since neither Elsa nor Fedora knew how long they had been submerged, they had no way of knowing exactly how much. Taking the new cylinders, they would be gambling their lives on an unknown quantity.

But now they had no alternative.

They swam back to the control room; slowly, because both were overwhelmingly aware of the need to husband what little air might be left to them. They changed the cylinders; Elsa to Meuvret's, Fedora to Moreno's. It wasn't difficult. Then they stared at each other through the expression-killing plastic of the masks. From now on, they were on borrowed time. They paddled silently back to that great useless rent in the U-boat's side.

It was, after all, a ten-inch gap. It was just on the cards that one of them, or both, might be able to wriggle through, at that place where the ripped steel gaped open the widest. What impeded them, of course, was the harness they carried and the cylinders themselves. In changing the cylinders, however, Fedora had had an idea; and now he saw that the idea might even work. It was a question of letting slip the cylinders, getting out through the hole, and then getting the equipment back on again, all without taking breath. Difficult, yes, but maybe possible. Elsa was slimmer than he was, though, and far more at home under water. So Elsa would have to try it first. . . .

He explained the idea to her by means of gesture, watching all the time the brown intelligent eyes behind the mica of her visor. When he had finished, she nodded and tapped him approvingly on the shoulder. For now it seemed that this was the only way. And so she positioned herself carefully, and breathed in deeply, and when her lungs were filled to the maximum she unbuckled the carrier and spat the nozzle of the air-tube from her mouth and let the equipment slide off her back into Johnny's waiting hands and thrust herself as hard as she could into the gaping steel mouth that instantly seemed to close over her head and shoulders.

. . . She nearly managed it. But not quite. For well over forty seconds, Fedora watched her body thrash and wriggle and wrestle in the water, her shoulders wedged as though inextricably in the cruel metal gap; then abruptly she tore herself backwards, pushed herself downwards, and Johnny caught her round the waist and slipped the air-tube into her mouth again. He felt her body shuddering against him as the air flooded back into her lungs, trembling from the pain of the salt sea water against her raw, steel-whipped shoulders and back. Vivid red scratches ran down almost to the points of her breasts, showing by how narrow a margin her attempt had failed, and the upper edges of her swimsuit had been shredded to ribbons. Johnny's own body twinged in sympathy as she writhed against his chest; he crushed her savagely against him, as though trying to kill her anguish by inflicting on her greater pain himself. The pain would hardly have mattered if she had got through. But she hadn't.

After a while, her muscles relaxed; Fedora hoisted the harness back on to her shoulders and they set off once

more for the control-room. Elsa was too cramped with
pain now to swim; he had to drag her along behind him
as best he could. And there for long minutes she rested,
directing the torch beam upwards while Johnny
attacked the conning-tower hatch, this time with an
iron crowbar. He worked slowly, using his remaining
energy in brief frenetic bursts. Yet at the end of his
efforts the heavy iron lid that held them prisoner was
barely even scratched.

Another quarter of an hour had gone by. Conning-
tower and escape cabin jammed, thought Fedora,
pausing to review once more the chain of abandoned
possibilities. Hole in the hull too small to get through.
Impossible to make it larger. And the minutes moving
past while he was thinking. It was no good. He wasn't
thinking at all. His brain just turned in circles. There'd
be very little air left now. No use. They'd had it. They
were screwed.

He swam down to Elsa, and for a few moments they
floated side by side, her arm across his waist. Behind the
impassive visor, her eyes were wrinkled up and there
were tears on her cheeks. Fedora wished exasperatedly
that there were some way of kissing her; it would be as
useful a way of passing the time as any other.

. . . Of passing the time. . . .

The small fishes moved inquisitively around them as
they floated, already as though lifeless, linked together
by their intertwined arms. Not far away were Moreno
and Meuvret, floating as they were floating but now
forever apart. Four corpses in a sunken U-boat; two of
them dead and two of them slowly dying. The end of
the affair. . . .

Johnny thought of those who had died already in this

grey steel tomb, of those who had drowned in a matter
of seconds as the bomb-ripped carcase had plunged to
the ocean floor. He thought of the skeleton on the bunk
and the skull on the table; all that remained of the crew,
of Hellman himself. The war had been almost over
when that bomb had dropped and Hellman had died;
Hellman's thoughts had also been of escape, of escape
from Europe to a new life in the Argentine. The U-boat
had sailed to carry him there, a long voyage across the
Atlantic, a flight from the destiny that would otherwise
have awaited him at Nuremberg; a fugitive ship, a
ghost ship; no guns, no shells, no torpedoes, just
provisions and loot. . . .

Elsa felt him suddenly stiffen in her arms, and raised
her head with an effort. Her eyes were hot now, her
brain muzzy, and for the last half-minute she had been
listening to the fast crescendo ticking of the blood in her
ears; certain signs that the air in her cylinder was
slowly failing. But now Fedora was tapping her shoulder
and turning away, ploughing himself downwards once
again towards the companionway passage. Too weary
now to use her arms, she pushed herself off from the
bulkhead and flippered her way painfully after him.
The movement made her head start pounding wildly
and her vision began to dim; she followed him closely,
blindly, well aware that whatever idea had occurred to
him represented their last and only chance. . . .

THEY broke the surface to a world not of air, as they had expected, but of light; a light so stunning in its intensity that at first all they could do was float on their backs and blink agonisedly through their misted visors at the wide blue vastness of the sky. Then they opened their mouths and let the warm sea air rush madly into their lungs, gulping in huge mouthfuls of it, while the sunlight hurtled down at them, swamping them in its radiance. To their left was the *Polarlys*, waiting silently, patiently; to their right, and at least a hundred yards nearer, was the long grey outline of a Navy corvette. Fedora heard a distant shout echoing from the bridge, and thought confusedly that the voice sounded rather like Trout's; he took Elsa under the shoulders and slowly, exhaustedly, they paddled towards safety.

The boarding-net came down with a rush as they approached. Mounting it cost Elsa the last remaining fragments of her energy; she stepped over the rail on to the deck, turned towards the *Polarlys* and saw with a sudden clarity the lonely figure of Feramontov at the stern staring towards her, his hands resting on his hips, the sea breeze ruffling his fair hair. She took another step forward, and one of the watching seamen caught her as she collapsed.

"Well, fancy meeting *you* here," said Trout. "Welcome aboard."

Fedora rested his weight on the guardrail, let sea water dribble out of his mouth. "It's all right," he said uncertainly. "Moreno's dead."

"Yes, I thought perhaps he might be," said Trout.

THE hotel window looked out on the steeply-angled slope of the Rock. Below were blue flowers and bougainvillea, the concrete quays and grey ships of the harbour; in the distance, red and brown, the Spanish coast, the low hills behind Algeciras. It all still seemed to Fedora slightly unreal. Only the faint chirping of the cicadas seemed familiar. Macfarlane sat in the easy chair and smoked his pipe and watched Fedora with his usual air of polite but uncomprehending concern.

"They'll fly her to England, of course," he said, "as soon as she's fully recovered. The boys from the Department will have to put her through the hoops. You realise that?"

"They won't get much out of her," said Johnny "Valera couldn't."

"No," said Macfarlane thoughtfully. "I don't suppose our Spanish friends are going to be very pleased about Valera. He was rather a good man, in his way."

"They're getting the Hellman papers, aren't they? —with the compliments of Her Majesty's Government. What more do they want?"

"Gibraltar, for one thing," said Macfarlane. "And your lady friend for another. They *did* arrest her, after all."

"Not on an extraditable offence. You're not suggesting that we should hand her back?"

"Oh no. It's just another reason why we want to get

her over to London as soon as we can. By the way, I've made it crystal clear in my report how extremely useful she's been. I think I can guarantee that she'll be shown every courtesy . . . perhaps even offered employment. Though as to that last, I can't be sure."

"Valera offered *me* every courtesy. It didn't pay."

"All the same—"

"And she doesn't want employment. Not of that kind."

"You seem very sure."

"To hell with the Department, anyway," said Johnny. He gave up looking out of the window. There was nothing there he hadn't seen before. He tried looking at the ceiling, instead. Nothing there, either. He got up. "I think I'll be going."

"There was just one thing," said Macfarlane, "I wanted to ask you."

"What?"

"You never explained just how you *did* get out of that damned U-boat."

Johnny's eyes focused, as though in pain, on the pipe in Macfarlane's hand. The last chance is always a hateful thing to think about. Especially when . . . you can't *explain* it, that's the trouble. When it's something so simple and obvious. You just can't explain what happens to your brains when you're trapped sixty feet under water, how it is that the simple and obvious things disappear from sight and there's nothing left but panic or a dull resignation to death. . . .

"The torpedo tubes," he said. "Manually operated. Opened quite easily. What we did was, we got out through the tubes."

He looked back with one hand on the doorknob.

"By the way," he said, "your pipe's gone out."

H E walked down the corridor to his room. Elsa was there, sitting on the bed; upswept hair and silver-varnished nails, trim as a kitten; wearing a dress and jacket of grey-and-white checked wool. "What are you doing here?" said Johnny, mildly surprised.

"Waiting for you. Why, what's the matter?"

"Nothing. It's the first time I've seen you with all your clothes on, that's all. You look very elegant."

"Shipboard life is so Bohemian. But one can't go everywhere wearing next to nothing."

"Oh, I approved of that as well." Johnny lifted the loose collar of her dress, ran his finger round inside the neck. The white scar tissue came into view, shiny and wrinkled; the burns were healing fast. He leant farther downwards to kiss her gently on the mouth. ". . . You still taste of salt," she said, "even after three days."

"Surely not, with all the whisky I've been drinking."

"You taste of that, too. It's been a long three days." She put an arm round his neck. "What do *I* taste of? Hospital?"

"I didn't notice," said Johnny. "I'll try again."

. . . After a time he felt her move, as though sleepily, in his arms. "Isn't this a *respectable* hotel?"

"Not with all these sailors about."

"And anyway, I thought you said you *liked* me dressed."

"Oh, shut up," said Fedora.

"All right, but that part unbuttons."

"Damn."

"*That's* right." Her head fell back on the pillows; her body uncurled slowly beside his. "Are you worried about anything? . . . Don't be."

"They're going to send you to England," said Fedora.

"It doesn't matter. Feramontov saw me on the ship. They know what happened. It won't be very long before they catch up with me. So I have to make the most of what I have left."

"Scared?"

"No. Not any more."

"That's right," said Fedora. "Don't be."